Enjoy these **PRIMROSE U.S.M.C.** titles from
R. Michael Haigwood

First Tour - Rescue
Second Tour - Suitcase
Third Tour - Sleeper Cell
Finders Keepers
Gilt
Squall
In the Name of Justice
Potbelly

Sal Sagev

R. Michael Haigwood

Printed in the United States of America

First Printing June 2022

ISBN 978-1-956661-21-7 Paperback

ISBN 978-1-956661-22-4 Hardcover

ISBN 978-1-956661-23-1 eBook

Published by: Book Services
www.BookServices.us

Contents

1. The Cabal ... 1
2. The File ... 17
3. Target ... 25
4. Team Meeting ... 37
5. Yancy Cowcatcher ... 47
6. Keno Game ... 57
7. Las Vegas ... 63
8. Search ... 83
9. The Connection ... 95
10. The Search ... 115
11. Boulder Dam Lodge ... 133
12. Allies ... 139
13. Sandy Valley ... 155
14. The Tail ... 165
15. The Stakeout ... 175
16. Yancy ... 183
17. Distribution ... 193
18. Red Bags ... 203
19. Mohammed ... 217
20. Money or Honor ... 233
21. Yancy ... 251
22. Hoover Dam ... 257
23. Temple Bar ... 265
24. The Pentagon ... 267
25. Cabal Headquarters ... 269

About the Author ... **273**

Sal Sagev

Thanks to those who gave inspiration for the characters:
   Terry Loveday, Doorman, Desert Inn Hotel
   Norman Lourenco, Valet Parking, Desert Inn Hotel
   Geno Ogden, Bellman, Desert Inn Hotel
   Larry Mortensen, Bell Captin, Tropicana Hotel
   Danny Mosco, Owner-Operator Limousine Service
   Brett Hern, Lt. Col. US Air Force—Special Ops
   Denise Ann Fuson Earl, American Indian
   Joe Roberts, US Navy

Thanks also to:

Betsy and Michael Feinberg —
   for all of your hard work.

Jean Santivasci —
   without whose help my books would still be
   in manuscript form, languishing on a shelf,
   unpublished.

"The world is a dangerous place, not because of those who do evil, but because of those who look on and do nothing"
Albert Einstein

Chapter One

The Cabal

The ten high-backed chairs were occupied by nine men and one woman, all dressed in tailored suits that fit without a wrinkle, even when seated. The spacious conference room was austere, with few furnishings other than the oversized table and a few unremarkable portraits. The sole woman sucked most of the light out of the room, radiating an aura of executive power and intelligence. A camouflaged smile on her beautiful face could only be detected by someone who knew her well.

The spokesman stood and directed his attention to the single chair parked in the center of the long, curved table across from the group. "Quintin Underwood Michaels," the man intoned. "We have an assignment that might interest you. As always, you may choose to make yourself available or not."

This wasn't the first time Quint had been seated in that same chair, listening to a new challenge from the suits across from him. He'd accepted many offers from the Cabal representatives in the past twenty years, and each one had been an experiment in terror. They had never offered him anything routine or mundane.

The faces in the suits had changed since his last visit, with the exception of the woman seated at the far right. He recognized the camouflaged smile, the twinkle in her eyes, the mischief showing through her corporate-controlled persona.

The gentlemen didn't introduce themselves, and Quint didn't expect them to. The lone woman didn't need an introduction.

She was known in their world as the best of the best. Sue Battle's reputation could be summed up in two words—consummate professional.

The spokesman continued, "The mission in the offering will require you to eliminate three known terrorists who are planning an attack on American soil. We will require your answer within twenty-four hours. The details will be provided by the young lady seated at the desk just outside the double doors."

Quint flashed back to his first meeting with the Cabal. He had been introduced to their vision of the world by a man in his winter years. The old man had sat alone behind a similar table, in the center chair, his face showing the wear of making decisions an ordinary citizen could never imagine making. The old man may have appeared frail, but one could see the passion in his eyes and the determination in his face, the face of a man used to winning, a man capable of taking on the evil of which he spoke.

"Young man, what are your feelings about the scum of the earth who are never punished for their diabolical and evil acts, their crimes against humanity?"

He didn't wait for an answer, but kept talking, never taking his eyes off Quint. "It is the Cabal's sincerest desire that evildoers receive the rewards they so richly deserve. We seek out those malignant, depraved citizens that others will not hunt down and prosecute because of political correctness, timidity, lack of funds, or intimidation by the evildoers themselves. The Cabal is not reluctant to cross borders to hunt down the bad guys.

"We ply our business under the radar when possible. Our scope is local or international, depending on the circumstances. Some countries give us a wink and a nod, others deter us, and some even pay us. We'll go to any extreme to accomplish the mission. Those who think they've gotten away with their wicked deeds will be surprised to find a shadow coming over them that they cannot shake."

The old man stopped to take a breath and asked, "What possessed you to seek us out? What motivates you?"

Quint thought back to his childhood and the defining act that sealed his quest for adventure. He answered the old man's question. "After this terrified little kid jumped from a railroad bridge into the Palouse River in Washington State, an unshakeable bug to discover his limits was born.

"When I was building special-order firearms in a gun shop, I met some of your people, and that led to my sitting here today. I was inspired by their stories of pulling the plug on criminals who had slipped through the cracks or had been intentionally released for political reasons.

"My motivation is to rid the world of the scum you're talking about. Political correctness has gone overboard, encouraging a hands-off approach to many who need to be dead."

The old man appeared to be pleased and with a quick smile retorted, "If you decide to sign a contract with us, you'll be that shadow I spoke of, and your first adventure, as you call it, could be south of the border."

Quint's introduction to the dark side of justice seemed like it was only yesterday.

Now the suits rose as a unit and filed out of the room through the big double doors. Quint remained seated for a minute.

He was wondering where he could find Sue when the double doors opened, and the young lady who'd escorted him into the chamber signaled him to follow her. That was all right with Quint; he had another look at her beautiful body as she led the way.

The young lady could have been a model but had chosen the Cabal, so Quint knew that as good looking as she was, her skills in mortal combat would be considerable. He would feel sorry for any young man who tried to make unwanted advances.

She handed Quint a folder. "Mr. Michaels, here's the information on the proposed assignment, and clipped on the cover is a note from Miss Battle."

She gave him a knowing wink and directed him to the front door, giving him the feeling of getting the bum's rush. "See you in the next day or so." She shook his hand with a firm grip and returned to her duties, her receding figure a stark contrast to the sparsely furnished hall.

The folder wasn't the first thing on his agenda. The note from Sue was his immediate interest. He peeled the envelope back and extracted a sheet of paper containing just two sentences.

QUINT
MEET ME AT THE STEAKHOUSE WE ENJOYED
THE LAST TIME.
EIGHT THIS EVENING.
SUE

The note was just like her: demanding, authoritarian, and to the point.

When her perfume had drifted across the conference table during the interview and attacked his memory banks, it had brought up vivid reflections of that candlelight dinner at the steakhouse a couple of years ago.

They'd crossed paths on numerous occasions, but until they were team members on a special mission, the fire that could be felt between them had remained at arm's length.

For her part, Sue had looked across the table at the only man she'd ever met who could give her tingly feelings that demanded attention without delay.

She could see his green eyes trying not to stare at her, but failing miserably, as enough electricity flowed between them to light up a small house. Sue knew the brown-haired, six-foot man could put out the fire raging within her. The memory of their last encounter had prompted her to write the short note for dinner.

Sue was raised by a career military officer. Her mother had passed away when Sue was a little child, leaving parental duties to her father alone. Being an only child and a military brat had set her on course to follow in the footsteps of her father, and she spent most of her youth training for that future. She learned martial arts, shooting, scuba, skydiving, rock climbing, and racing cars, along with the scholarly textbook work needed for a successful military career. When her father suggested one of the military academies for her continuing education, she resisted, saying it was a waste of time. She enlisted in the army, to his great displeasure. Because of her high IQ, Officer Candidate School gave her a commission three years before any of the academies would have.

The army career was short-lived. Frustrated at not being accepted as an equal in Special Forces led her to answer an ad placed by the Cabal. They were looking for experienced military people seeking adventurous employment. That was the catalyst for her many years as a field operative in the covert war on evil.

Quint, folder in hand, found his way back to the elevator that had brought him down to the meeting room. He'd always felt a little cramped in elevators, especially one that went below ground. Stepping into the empty lift, he pressed the lobby button and was relieved that the ride to the surface was short.

Exiting the building, he found the limo that had delivered him to the compound waiting. As usual, the driver leaned against the front fender, smoking. Quint figured the front-fender-smoking thing was a requirement for all limo drivers; they all seemed to fit the mold of Hollywood's characters.

As Quint approached the car, the driver dropped his cigarette, squashed the life out of it, and opened the door. "Where to, Mr. Michaels?"

"Back to the hotel. And by the way, is that steakhouse with the great wine cellar still open? The one you took me to a couple of years ago?"

"Yes sir. Would you like to drive by?"

"Yes. I need to make a dinner reservation."

As the limo accelerated through the gate, Quint was as enchanted as ever at the landscape of New Mexico, belying the desert image presented in the movies. Hollywood, it seemed, always put the country in a negative light, not in keeping with reality. The fantasy land of film tended to lean more toward the dark side.

Quint scanned the folder while the driver sped towards town, paying no attention to the posted speed limit.

The folder contained little more than twenty pages, direct and on point. But it would need to be studied in detail. It contained photos of his targets, along with a short profile of their past and present habits, quirks, and likely haunts within the city of Las Vegas.

He let out a slow whistle as he imagined the consequences of a terrorist attack at one of the many hotels on the Las Vegas Strip. Four of the largest hotels in the world were possible targets. So was the historic Hoover Dam on the Colorado river. Maybe even the largest jet fighter base in the world: Nellis Air Force Base. The list of targets was only limited by a terrorist's imagination.

If the terrorists could somehow damage the dam, it would flood the Imperial Valley in California, destroying all the crops that supplied the nation with fruits and vegetables. As a major power source, the damage would dim the lights in California, Arizona, and Nevada.

Any of the hotels hit on a Saturday morning would surely double the lives lost at the World Trade Center.

Quint's head was spinning with the possibilities.

Just as the spinning slowed and critical thinking began to form, the limo pulled up to the curb at the steakhouse. Quint rushed in and spoke to the hostess about dinner. He was flattered that she remembered him from past visits. The hostess smiled and put his reservations down for seven thirty.

They sped away again, not paying any attention to the speed limit, and arrived in short order at the hotel.

The driver jumped out and opened the door for Quint, saying, "Your hotel, Mr. Michaels. I'll be here when you're ready."

Quint handed the driver a double sawbuck.

Heading into the lobby, it occurred to Quint that this assignment was world-fucking serious.

He was wondering why the local fuzz, FBI, CIA, and every other abbreviated department wasn't in on the hunt. Or maybe they were, but the dots hadn't yet been connected?

No matter, he'd do his part to take down any low-lifes who would dare to hit the United States again.

Bypassing the elevator, he bounded up the two flights of stairs to his room. Once inside, he picked up the landline and put in a call to his gun store in Blaine, Washington.

"Gun Shop, Jake speaking. How may I help you?"

Quint could see his friend and trusted partner in the war on evil standing behind the display case in the front of the shop. Jake Dahl's six-foot-two-inch frame was thin, his hair blond and usually a mess. He kept his mustache neatly trimmed. His blue eyes had a kindly look, but they could turn to ice in a second.

"Jake, Quint here. I met with the Cabal people and I have the package. I'll let you know what I think when I return. I'm having dinner with Sue this evening. Anything new in the real world?"

"No, same ol', same ol.'"

"Okay, see you in a couple of days."

Quint was happy he hired Jake a few years ago to assist in the gun shop. He'd been a sniper with Special Forces. A guy couldn't have a more trusted friend.

On their many missions together, Jake had proven his skills in any environment and under any conditions. He'd made a regular habit of pulling their fat out of the fire.

Quint peered out the window of his room to see the limo driver leaning on the front fender, smoking, waiting for him to come down.

It was time to head over to the steakhouse and meet Sue—a delicious thought.

He avoided the elevator again, using the stairs, which were quicker anyway, regardless of his aversion to the confined space of the lift.

Upon seeing Quint, the driver crushed his butt and said, "Good evening, Mr. Michaels. Shall we hit the road?"

"Yes, let's hit the road," Quint replied. "And be quick about it. We're running a tad late, which will set off a firestorm from the beautiful redhead who awaits."

The driver, obviously a gifted throttle jockey, slipped through the traffic with ease, arriving five minutes ahead of schedule.

At the curb near the front door, Quint remarked, "Damn, if I ever need a driver with your skills, I'll be calling on you. Sorry, I didn't get your name last time."

"Jesse, Jesse Thomas Turbo at your service, Mr. Michaels. And by the way, I don't accept tokes. I'll put the double sawbuck you gave me in a donation box somewhere. We're all pros here.

It hadn't occurred to Quint that the driver was anything more than a highly skilled chauffeur. He was a little embarrassed about his assumption. He should have known better. The Cabal would have all their bases covered, with professionals in every slot.

"Sorry, Jesse. My mistake."

"Not a problem, Mr. Michaels. I try to play my role to the best of my ability. I'm supposed to keep you out of trouble while you're here. In the future, if you need an extra hand, give me a call."

Quint stepped out of the limo and headed into the restaurant. Looking back, he said, "I'll give you a call in the morning."

"I'll be at your service. After I take you to the airport I won't be responsible for you any longer. Don't forget to keep me in mind for something more than limo driving."

"Thanks, Jesse, see you tomorrow."

The car pulled away from the curb, heading in the direction of the Cabal compound. Jesse honked and waved out the window as he disappeared down the street, as before, paying no mind to the speed limit.

The hostess directed Quint to the table he and Sue had shared on their last visit. It was in the corner near the fireplace, barely visible from the hostess desk.

Sue waved to get his attention. As he approached, he saw that Sue was about to stand and greet him, but he put his hand on her shoulder and bent over, whispering in her ear, "You'd better stay seated. If we hug, there'll be a show here that will be talked about for years to come."

Sue whispered back, "I agree. I'll stay in the chair for now, but the fire rages within. It will need attention soon. We may just settle for drinks and then head for the barn."

"Sue—"

"No business talk tonight, Quint."

"What I had in mind wouldn't require any verbal conversation. Are we going to order dinner or go put the fever out?"

Sue grabbed her handbag and said, "My car's out back!"

Quint could smell the coffee brewing as he opened his eyes to the familiar surroundings of Sue's bedroom.

The sound of the shower filtered its way through to the kitchen as he poured a cup of her excellent coffee. A smile came to his face as bits and pieces of last night's uninhibited lovemaking came to mind, when they tried to put out the flames that shot up every time they touched.

"Pour me a cup," Sue yelled from the bathroom. "I'll be right out. Black, no sugar. You have thirty minutes before your ride gets here. I made arrangements for them to pick you up here."

Quint shook his head and marveled at her attention to details. He'd never thought of calling Jesse to come here to pick him up, and he would have been late for his flight.

He took Sue her coffee and traded places with her in the shower, not touching, for fear of kindling another bout of the insatiable appetite that smouldered between them.

Quint could barely see her through the fog in the shower, as she said, "You could get hired on by any fire department in the country. Call me when you've studied the file. I have some information that came up after it was written."

Quint glanced out the window to see Jesse leaning on the limo's fender as before, the cigarette smoke curling up from his left hand.

He wasn't a big man, maybe five-ten, one eighty, crew cut with a handlebar mustache.

He was obviously in good physical condition—as all the Cabal people were. There was the telltale sign of a handgun under the upper portion of his blazer, and if one could see under his clothing, there would be another weapon of some sort for backup.

Stepping out, Quint nodded to Jesse. "How are things this morning?"

"Fine," Jesse answered as he held the door open.

As they sped away from the curb, Quint asked, "Jesse, how did you happen to hook up with the Cabal?"

"It's a long story, but I can give you the short version. With eight years in the Navy, four of which were with Special Operations, I decided to give civilian life a chance. That didn't work out. After the adrenalin of being a Navy SEAL and in Special Ops, I had to find something to feed my appetite for adventure. I came across an ad in the paper inserted by a company looking for former military people to sign on for some additional excitement.

"So here I am. Nothing dramatic, like running away from the law or being chased by a woman with something permanent in mind."

"Is the limo thing a steady assignment, or have you been on other more risky ventures?"

"I've been south of the border, and I've been in the Middle East."

Quint followed up, "Why were you chosen for those particular areas?"

There was a pause before Jesse replied, "I speak Spanish and various dialects of Farsi. I'm also an explosives expert. I come from a family of chemists. I didn't want to follow them into the laboratory."

As Jesse eased the car into the airport drop-off area, Quint said, "I'll keep you in mind if anything comes up in your field."

Jesse opened the door and handed Quint his bag. "I think I retrieved all your things from the hotel. Sue didn't give me much notice. I hope to see you down the road, Mr. Michaels."

"Call me Quint, Jesse."

"Okay, Quint. This limo gig is getting a little boring. Don't forget me."

The limousine pulled away from the curb with a honk and a wave, a cigarette butt flying from Jesse's hand, the tires squealing.

As Quint walked up to the ticket agent, thoughts of last night crossed his mind again. He couldn't get the beautiful redhead out of his mind. There was so much energy packed into her five-foot-five frame, a ball of fire ready to explode, her green eyes matching his with desire. The body of a model hid the fury that could be unleashed at the drop of a hat when the need for action against the bad guys presented itself.

The ticket agent brought him back to the real world. "Hello, may I help you?"

Quint smiled and put away his memories for another time. "Yes, thank you."

Chapter Two

The File

Going through the package from the Cabal made the flight to Sea-Tac airport seem short. From Seattle, Quint decided to take the ferry to Anacortes and then on to Blaine by car. He wanted the extra time on the ferry to study the package. It was relatively brief, but the implications of a major hit in the United States required attention to every small detail.

He'd taken some important missions before, but this one would have world-shaking consequences if he were not successful. The ferry ride gave him time to study, and the more he read, the scarier it became.

He paused from time to time to look up and enjoy the succulent greenery of the Northwest. From the border of California to Canada there was some of the most breathtaking scenery in the country. The Puget Sound and the Strait of Juan de Fuca possessed the most beautiful inland waterways in the world.

Docking at the Port of Anacortes, Quint rented a car and drove the scenic Chuckanut Drive route that followed the inland waterways to Bellingham. From there it was little more than twenty miles to the border town of Blaine, where his gun shop was located. The shop sat between a restaurant and a bike rental store on the main street through town. The view from the shop looked more like a Norman Rockwell painting than the scene of a real-world abandoned cannery, an assortment of fishing boats, and a marina where all types of vessels from around the world were docked. Blaine was noted for the International Peace Arch on its border, expressing the rapport the two nations of Canada and America had enjoyed for hundreds of years.

Quint parallel parked two spaces down from the gun shop. He entered the restaurant and waved at the proprietor. "How about some donuts and coffee to go?"

With his purchase in hand, Quint walked next store and gazed in his shop window. Jake was chatting with a customer while shouldering a shotgun, demonstrating its handling qualities.

Jake was an expert gunsmith on every make and model of firearm known to man. He had become known in the covert world as one of the best, someone Quint trusted with his life.

Quint moved from the window to the front door. As he entered the friendly atmosphere, he was thankful he had a place to call home. Setting the coffee and donuts on the counter, he told Jake and the customer to help themselves.

"Nice shotgun, Jake. Is it new in the inventory?"

"Yessiree Bob. It came UPS yesterday, and our friend here is going to take it before we even get a good look at it."

Quint smiled. "Enjoy the shotgun." He retreated through the doorway to his office behind the counter. Jake finished up the sale and joined Quint.

Jake put the file down and remarked, "This is it? They're not giving us much. Telling us there are two Middle East types loose in Vegas, two photos taken some time ago of two men who later arrived on a private airstrip somewhere in southern Nevada with the knowledge and resources to bring down a five-thousand room hotel. Where the hell do we start?"

Quint asked, "Did you finish the upstairs renovation?"

"Yes."

"And the workshop in the back?"

"It is exactly as you requested. No one but you, me, and the contractor would be able to find the hidden door. The interior's been modified to your specifications. I must say, the shop is a gunsmith's dream."

Quint nodded and led the way up to the second floor, walking by the huge bay window overlooking the scenic harbor that always gave him a sense of calmness, an almost hypnotic feeling of tranquility. The fishing fleet and private yachts rolled calmly as the tide ebbed out to sea.

Standing at the huge window, Quint said, "Jake, we start with what we know. Two men, maybe more, are loose in Las Vegas. They mean to take down a hotel or other viable targets. There are many to choose from in that desert community. They'll have to purchase tell-tale equipment and thus leave a paper trail. They may start out invisible, but their journey will reveal signs we'll be looking for. We have many avenues to follow, but first things first. Tomorrow we'll rent a plane and fly down to Vegas and get started. For now, let's take a look at the hidden room."

"Okay, follow me."

Jake walked around the end of the counter and through the door to the gunsmithing area. He pulled the horn of a stuffed buffalo head over the workbench and the back wall rotated, exposing a room filled with the latest technology available in the world of covert operations.

Quint whistled. "Wow! One hell of a job, Jake."

"I thought you might like it. What we have at our immediate disposal is the state of the art for anything we could possibly want or need. We have combined our best with the best of others in our field. It's all here."

"That reminds me, have you heard from Jett Horn?"

"No. The last I heard he was still down in Belize."

Quint said, "I think we should give him a ring, and see if he wants to have a hand in our search-and-destroy mission on the bad guys. His experience, language skills, and appearance would be invaluable. He can mingle at the local watering holes where our targets and their ilk will be hanging out."

As they toured the newly remodeled hidden room, Jake remarked, "I've updated my pilot's license to include multi-engine and instrument ratings. I'm in good graces with the owner of the flight school. He has several planes that would meet our needs. They are for rent, lease, sale, or charter. I can check with him about a charter, if you like."

Quint's eyebrows arched. "I'm taking it for granted that you'll be acquiring something you've flown before, so we won't be practicing?"

Jake winked with his one good eye and responded, "I'm really good for a guy with one eye. Of course I'm better at shooting, since a scope only requires one good peeper."

Quint smiled, put his hands up in defense, and replied, "My last flight in a small aircraft was an experience I'd rather not go through again. When we landed the plane was out of fuel and full of bullet holes."

"You know, come to think of it, Jett's plane would be perfect."

"If he's willing to join us, we could take all our weapons and not worry about losing a charter. Who knows, we might wind up using the plane for a fighter or bomber. Let's wait until we talk with Jett before you check out a charter."

Quint punched in Jett's number in Belize. He could picture his diving on the barrier reef there. He was the all-American type—five-eleven, two-ten, black and hazel, good athlete. His background was Army Special Forces, Navy SEAL, and National Security Agency, as well as a tour with drug enforcement south of the border. And of course a standout with the Cabal.

After the fifth ring a woman's voice answered, *"Hola, buenos dias."*

Quint countered, *"¿Hablas inglés?"*

The woman replied, *"Si, hablo un poco de inglés."*

Trying to remember his Spanish, Quint replied, "Jett Horn, *por favor.*" He'd made a similar call a few months back and enticed Jett into joining their last mission for the Cabal, which had brought down four dictators to the benefit of the free world.

There was a pause on the other end as the woman yelled out something Quint didn't understand.

Finally Jett came on. *"¿Cómo estás?,* Quint?"

"Well, is the Spanish lesson over, Jett? I thought Belize spoke English."

"I hire my assistants where I can find them."

Quint inquired, "Do you have a few minutes to hear about an exciting adventure?"

"Quint, if the adventure you're shopping is like the last time, count me missing. Out of the nine lives I had, your sense of adventure has used up four of them, and I carelessly exploited two on other occasions."

"Don't throw in the towel just yet. Hear me out."

Quint could hear a sigh of frustration from Jett. "Okay, dazzle me with the patriotic line about how I need to stand tall for my country."

"You must be reading my mind, Jett. That's exactly what is needed here. We have a couple of bad guys on the loose in Las Vegas. They have the know-how to bring down a major hotel. Maybe Hoover Dam. We need your ever-so-brilliant mind and world-class experience."

"Okay, Quint, don't go overboard with the atta-boy shit. What can I do?"

"You could embed with the local Middle East culture there."

"You're not convincing me. There are a lot of guys with my skills."

"I don't trust anyone else. Besides, you owe me and Jake. As you recall, we pulled your fat out of the fire last time."

"Shit."

"Sorry I had to pull that card, but we need you."

"What else is on your mind, Quint? I know you very well."

"Well, there is one other thing. Do you still have that cool airplane? The one we used on the last go around?"

"Oh, so that's it. My skills don't mean shit. You just want to use my plane!"

"Don't be so negative, Jett."

"I suppose you also need me to pilot?"

"That would help, but no. Jake upgraded his certificates."

"I suppose you are suggesting my plane and me will not be in any serious danger, and I will be handsomely compensated?"

"No guarantees."

After a long silence, Jett said, "Well, I am a little bored right now. What's on the agenda?"

Quint gave a sigh of relief. "Jett, our funds are unlimited, but I'm sure you wouldn't be doing this just for the money. This is by-God serious shit. If you were ever inclined to be a patriot and support your country without the expectations of financial reward, this is the time."

"Okay, okay! Jesus, Quint! Save the rah rah shit and fill me in."

"If you'll fly up to Bellingham, we'll meet you there and then drive up to the gun shop in Blaine. We can plan the mission there. We need to do this like yesterday."

"How about I fly up tomorrow evening?"

"Give us a call when you touch down."

Chapter Three

Target

Najib turned to yell at Mahathir over the roar of the twin-engine plane. "You have to improve your English. Slow down and speak clearly. We can't afford any misinterpretation of our instructions. The pilot's name is Yancy, not Nancy. You look sick, Mahathir."

Mahathir, sitting in the back of the four-seater, yelled back, "We weren't meant to fly. We should only leave the earth when we're on our way to paradise. I'll not fly again. Those who flew before were true heroes. When they flew, they were on their way to paradise, unlike us, who are going to land. We should fly this contraption into the nearest building and begin our journey to the promised land. I'm going to lose my breakfast."

Najib laughed at his friend and said, "There are no buildings. The plane is flying over the desert. Use the bag behind the seat there."

The pilot could understand what the two were saying, but couldn't care less. The money was too good to pass up, and it was sure safer than flying dope. He was used to aviating people who didn't speak English well, but most were of Spanish descent. His plane was for hire, no questions asked. The fees for his services were outrageous, but worth it. Not giving a shit about who, what, or where had paid off over the years.

He'd had dealings with Middle Eastern types before. He didn't cotton to them, but their money was as good as any. He charged the two airheads double his regular rate. They didn't even blink at the astronomical fee for the short flight over the border to Nevada.

Yancy Cowcatcher came from a long line of cattle rustlers, but those days were long gone. He had decided to spend his time in the air. He joined the U.S. Air Force at seventeen, and after twenty years of faithful service, he retired to live his dream: contract pilot. The past ten years had led him from South America to Africa and Europe. Money being his only motivation had kept all the head games out of his life. He'd decided long ago that sides didn't matter. In his mind everyone was evil, each guy as evil as the next. When something touched him down deep in the recesses of his soul, he looked the other way. He kept those feelings at arm's length, so they wouldn't interfere with his financial goals.

Yancy could fit into almost any crowd north or south of the border. He stood six foot plus, with brown hair, brown eyes, and a dark complexion. He was quick to smile and had a gift for gab. He looked over at the apparent leader of the two and asked, "It's time to give me the new heading. What's with all the secrecy? I'll know where we are when we land. Just tell me where the hell you want me to bring her down, and we can get on with the program."

Najib responded, "You are being paid a very good fee for your services. Please fly the plane as I tell you." He handed Yancy a piece of paper with the latest heading.

Yancy thought, *These guys are as nervous as a combat engineer deciding whether to cut the red wire or the green one.* Looking at the paper, he knew exactly where they wanted to set down. It was a small desert community about forty-five miles south of Las Vegas, in a valley on the California-Nevada border.

He'd landed there once before to deliver some questionable characters and their small cargo of brown boxes. He didn't ask and didn't want to know what they contained. The flight paid well and it was one way.

He remembered the main tarmac was void of pot holes and well maintained. Flowing out from the tarmac were paved streets used by the residents to idle up to their homes—incorporated into hangars. He didn't have a problem landing there and being rid of the two jittery assholes. If he'd been paid in advance, he might have been tempted to dump the two out along the way.

This flying community numbered nearly a hundred aircraft and a head count close to one hundred and fifty. There was no tower or night landing lights, so the airfield was limited to day use, unless of course you could get enough of the residents to light the tarmac with their headlights.

"When will we arrive at our destination?" asked Najib. "Mahathir is very ill. We need to put the airship down."

Yancy thought about opening the right side door and rolling just enough to expel Najib and then Mahathir, but responded, "We are about fifteen minutes out. Hopefully, your friend won't die before then. It would require a huge amount of paperwork, so keep him alive until I set down."

"Yancy, with your unusually high fees, I think you shouldn't be so rude. I get the feeling you dislike me and my friend. Do you have a dislike for people from the Middle East?"

"I don't like anyone or anything. My only interest in this world, Najib, is money. Nothing else matters—you, your friend, or anyone else. It matters not to me where you're from; I couldn't care less. Reading the daily news from your part of the world would lead one to believe you two might be up to no good. But it's none of my business. As soon as we land, and you take leave of my plane, I'll be on my way. You, my friend, will be a distant memory. I'll say again, I have no interest in your affairs."

Mahathir whispered to Najib in their native tongue, *"We need to kill this infidel. He's a sarcastic pig."*

Najib answered, *"I was thinking of doing just that, but I can't fly this thing, so we'll have to wait until we land. He is a typical money-hungry Westerner. When our transportation is near the plane I'll shoot him. We'll be in town before anyone checks out the plane, and there are no records for anyone to discover us. It will be a pleasure to kill this capitalist pig."*

Yancy was laughing to himself at the whispered conversation between the two passengers, who didn't know he could hear them, let alone understand their language.

Before he landed, he would perform a couple of belly rolls, and they would get airsick, incapable of doing anything but wishing for solid ground. He would put them out, take whatever money they had, and leave them.

When Yancy could see the desert airstrip off in the distance, he began to rock and roll the plane. Within minutes the two were pea-green and wanting to puke their guts out.

Yancy made a three-point landing in a place called Sandy Valley, Nevada.

Najib yelled, "Are you crazy?" and hastily leaned forward, trying not to upchuck. Yancy was happy that he didn't. He idled over to the maintenance hangar and brought the plane to a stop.

Jumping out, Yancy ran around and helped the two dizzy, airsick scumbags down to the tarmac, where he cuffed them to a fuel truck. Not paying any attention to their protests, he set their bags down and searched them for cash. To his surprise, one bag was full of Yankee C-notes. Smiling at his good fortune, Yancy threw the bag into the cockpit, waved at the sick duo, and climbed into the plane. He took off with a smile, dipping his wings as a farewell gesture.

The limo pulled up to the maintenance hangar, the driver expecting to find his passengers ready for a ride to town, not handcuffed to a fuel truck. The local service attendant had just arrived, and he was trying to get the cuffs off without success.

The limo driver had been in the business for years in Vegas and always kept handcuffs and keys in his glove box for emergencies. He'd dealt with many strange people over the years and took the situation in stride, not asking any questions as he released his airsick passengers.

Speaking in his native language, Najib, said, "*We will hunt that infidel down and behead him after we take care of business. He will be painstakingly tortured for his treachery before we separate his head from his body.*"

The limo driver offered them water and opened the door. He didn't understand their words, but it was obvious they were fit to be tied.

Mahathir said, "Please take us to our hotel."

Keno Game looked at the two pathetic individuals and wondered what the hell they'd done to have someone cuff them and fly off.

"Gentlemen, I wasn't informed of your destination, only where to pick you up."

Keno was a long-time Vegas resident, having worked in most of the hotels on the Strip in nearly every department before buying into the limo service, and he was finally in the chips. He owned the company, but drove most of the unusual or high-profile requests to keep an eye on things. This one was in the unusual category.

Keno had always used his short height as an asset. Being only five-foot five, led people to overlook him and his capabilities. He shaved his head and wore a goatee to enhance his shortness, but he couldn't hide his piercing blue eyes unless he wore shades. To keep his all-around abilities under wraps, he didn't brag on his martial arts skills in ju-jitsu, karate, and boxing. He'd worked for a time as a bodyguard to the rich and famous, and he incorporated those skills into his limo business. He was known around town as Keno because in his early days he'd been a keno writer and player. Game was a family name, so it fit well with Keno.

Najib looked at the short, baldheaded driver and dismissed him as a credible threat. *"Mahathir, our driver seems to be a bit of a knucklehead, as they say in English. We might continue to use him as needed."*

Keno wasn't sure, but he got the feeling they were talking about him. He thought it best to keep his real identity as owner of the limo service to himself. He would play the role of a driver with little or no interest in his surroundings, wanting only to please his fare.

Najib said, "Driver, we are staying at the Strat. Please take us there."

Keno thought, *Damn, what an arrogant asshole! It will be hard to keep from bitch slapping these two cocksure punks. If nothing else, they fit the profile of Middle East terrorist types. I think I'll keep tabs on them, whether they continue to use my service or not.*

Keno put the window up behind his seat and turned on the mics in the passenger area of the limo. He could hear a lot of gibberish, but didn't understand a word. His view in the rearview mirror revealed that the two were agitated, their arms saying as much as their mouths.

The drive over the twisting, narrow road of Columbia Pass didn't seem to bother the two nerds; they must have been used to lousy roads wherever they came from.

Once they hit the freeway, it was a short ride at eighty miles an hour to the gaming capital of the world, the limo blending in with the heavy Los Angeles traffic heading to Vegas to hit the big one. The casinos were happy to accommodate their ambitions for a quick score.

Turning off I-15 onto Russell Road, Keno took a left on Las Vegas Boulevard for a tour of the Strip, and the passengers stopped yelling at each other to look out the windows as the limo passed the most famous sign in the world: *Welcome to Las Vegas*. The road was crowded with picture-happy people causing a minor traffic jam. One of the passengers pointed at the sign and made a gesture of cutting one's throat, which sent a chill up Keno's spine. He thought, *These guys might really be here to do some damage.*

After slowing to let his riders gawk at the hotels on the Strip, Keno pulled into the Strat, where the doorman yelled to his friend to pull up to the curb next to the baggage handlers, who were eager to help anyone in one of Keno's limos. They were disappointed to find the passengers didn't have any luggage to speak of and shunned any assistance.

Najib said, as he exited the limo, "I'll expect you to pick us up here tomorrow morning at seven."

Keno nodded to the SOB and handed him one of his cards to be sure they didn't lose his phone number. He wanted to keep track of their whereabouts, and there was no better way than to be their driver.

Keno shook hands with the doorman and baggage handlers and said, "Sorry about those two pukes. Maybe you guys could let me know when they leave the hotel or if they have visitors." He gave them a double sawbuck apiece and bid them farewell. He would come back prior to their pickup time in the morning and speak with the bellmen who roomed them to find out what their room numbers were. A Jackson greenback would help the bellman remember the two and keep him informed of their movements in the hotel.

Yancy Cowcatcher got a tingly feeling in his spine every time his mind wandered to his drop-off in Sandy Valley. Those two SOBs might be up to no good, but they would have to wire home for more money. The bag he relieved them of contained over a quarter of a million in Yankee dollars. When he opened the bag, he almost lost control of the plane. *Jesus, were they gamblers or bagmen for some mafia people?* They could pass for Russians, but they hadn't been speaking Russian. So he figured they were terrorists. The catch was that if he reported his drop-off to the proper authorities, he'd have to give up the money, which would get lost in the dark, deep hole of the government bureaucracy and be of no use to anyone. He could make better use of the money himself.

Yancy was in a quandary: Should he go back on his faithful adherence to his policy of not giving a shit or listen to the little voice telling him there was something wrong with this picture?

Was there a time when his country came first, not his greed for more money than he could not possibly spend in his lifetime?

That little feeling of guilt way down deep was becoming a problem. He'd tried to shake it off, but those two he'd dropped off in the valley kept coming back to him. They had a look of hate and determination in their eyes. When he'd cuffed them, the look they gave him was not one of just being duped. It was pure venom.

Yancy dialed in a heading for Yuma, Arizona, where he had picked up the two lowlifes. He knew a man in Yuma who could identify any bogus money that might be in the bag. There could also be a chance of finding out where the two had sprouted from.

Damn, this tugging of conscience is way harder than not giving a shit.

Keno parked his pickup across the street from the Strat, not wanting to draw any attention to himself.

Entering the front door and drifting through the casino to the bell desk, he spoke to the captain on duty. They had known each other for years, even though business was their only connection.

"Hello Keno, how's business?" The captain's attitude was strictly business.

Bell captains were not Keno's favorite people.

"Business is good, thanks." He slipped the captain a C-note. "I need some information on a couple of guys I dropped off here yesterday. Two Middle East types, with angry looks and demeanor. Do you or maybe one of the bellmen recall what rooms they are in?"

The bell captain responded, "Not hard to remember those two surly jerks. They gave the bellman a bad time, telling him they didn't need assistance, and stiffed him. And it was only five minutes later they came back to the lobby, looking for the bellman because they couldn't find their rooms. He took them up to the ninth floor and pointed them down the hall. They stiffed him again."

The captain was willing to help; aside from the C-note motivating him, he clearly had a genuine dislike for the new hotel guests.

Keno said, "I would be interested to know if they have any visitors, rent a car, or anything that seems unusual to you."

The captain smiled. "Not a problem, Keno. I'll spread the word around to keep an eye on them."

Mohammed spoke slowly into the phone. "It would be better if we are not seen together. I have secured you employment with a cleaning company that disinfects hotel kitchens. You'll have access to nearly all the hotels on the Strip at one time or another.

"I'll come to the hotel this evening and give you the details. We have little time to get things going. Our goal is to take down a major hotel on the anniversary of the twin towers."

Najib said, "Come to room 911."

He closed the cell without a salutation.

Chapter Four

Team Meeting

Jake was looking in the display case, helping a young lady who was interested in a small handgun for her purse. He asked, "Have you any experience with firearms?"

Before she could reply, the wall phone jingled. Jake excused himself and picked up the receiver. "The Gun Shop. How may I help you?"

There was a short pause as he listened to the caller. Nodding his head, he said, "Sure, I'll tell Quint. See you in a few."

He returned to helping the young lady, showing her a small Colt .380 auto. She liked the feel of the pistol and thought she might make a purchase.

Jake asked again, "Do you have any experience with handguns?"

"No. I would like to take a class on the handling of weapons."

While Jake was explaining the firearms course, Quint came up to the counter from the back room and asked, "I hope that was Jett on the phone?"

Jake turned away from the small, attractive woman with jet black straight hair and answered, "It was. He'll rent a car and drive up from Bellingham."

Quint replied, "Are you going to sell my favorite .380?"

"Yes. I believe our friend here is going to take the Colt and our firearms course. It might be a challenge, since she only has one good eye, though she said the patch was just temporary from recent routine surgery."

When all the government forms were completed, and the sale was finally concluded, Jake told the woman if all went well she could take possession in a couple of days. In the meantime she could enroll in the firearms class. The young lady agreed to sign up and paid cash for the pistol. With a handshake that most men would find a challenge, she left the store.

Quint asked Jake, "Have you seen her before?"

"No."

"Did you notice her hands were not the least bit nervous handling the .380? She is not a novice with guns. I believe the woman had more than pistols on her mind. Did she share her name?"

Jake looked over the background application and answered, "Bernice Pearl, black, brown, five-five, one forty. Address is General Delivery, Blaine, Washington. Not much to learn from that."

Quint looked puzzled. "She wasn't here for the Colt. There was something else. We'll see what the lady's background check reveals. And you know, Jake, she could be telling the truth about the patch, but consider this. If she has heterochromic eyes, all she has to do is switch the patch to the other side, and bingo, the perp will have the wrong description."

"Heterochromic?" asked Jake.

"Yeah. Like my Uncle Charlie. He had one brown eye and one blue eye."

"But Bernice Pearl has to know how in depth the background check is," suggested Jake.

As they pondered the customer's real reason for shopping in the gun store, the wall phone jingled again. Jake picked up and was about to repeat his standard greeting when he was cut off by a familiar voice.

"Jake, this is Sue."

Jake handed the phone to Quint, and smiled. "It's your favorite redhead."

"Quint here."

"Quint, my plane will arrive at Sea-Tac this evening. I'll spend the night in Seattle and drive up tomorrow afternoon. I have some new information you'll find disturbing. We have three, not two, bad guys in Vegas. One has been in deep cover for at least four years. Our information source expired before he could give us a complete outline of their intentions. The pictures you have are confirmed to be the two who arrived by private plane. We don't have a description of the third party. It will be a serious challenge to locate the three terrorists before they strike."

Quint's jaw began to grind, thinking about how to find an individual without a description in a city of two million. He replied, "Sue, was there any information on their timetable?"

"Quint, it's near the end of August now, so I would suggest they're aiming for a hit date on the anniversary of the twin towers, which means we don't have much time."

Quint replied, "Jett will arrive about the same time as you do. We can gather at the shop, put our heads together, and figure out how to attack the problem. Jett has offered his plane for our trip to Vegas.

All that aside, how about dinner and dancing one night before we have to put those inclinations on ice? We'll head over to that specialty seafood place on Birch Bay."

Sue, her smile almost detectable over the landline, said, "Sounds good to me. See you tomorrow."

Sue could see Quint on the other end of the line and smiled again as she replaced the receiver. She would enjoy putting the world's problems on hold for an evening of dining and dancing with the one man who could put the fire out that burned within her. He knew where to take her and how to keep her on the edge until the volcano erupted.

Jake put the closed sign in the front window of the shop and locked the door. The team had assembled in the hidden room and didn't want to be disturbed. The locals were accustomed to the shop closing at odd hours. It was a pattern set since the shop opened and common knowledge that the owners had other interests.

He made sure the security cameras were on before following the rest of the gang into the clandestine war room.

Quint was the first to speak as they took their seats around the table used to repair and build exotic weapons for black ops around the world.

"Ladies and gentlemen."

Quint was interrupted by Sue. "I'm surely a lady, but I think you paint with a broad brush to call the rest of this motley crew gentlemen."

There was a round of laughter, for they all knew Sue was a lady of the first order, but she could turn deadly at the drop of a hat when action required it. Her humor was taken as intended—to break the ice for a serious meeting.

"Shall I continue? Jett, Jake, and I are happy you could join us, Sue. As you know, we have a world-class situation on our hands. And I understand you have some additional information to share since we left the Cabal headquarters. You're up."

Sue tossed a folder to each of them. She remained sitting. Opening her folder, she directed the others to follow suit.

"Most of what you see is old news. However, there is some speculative news about the two bad guys who landed somewhere in southern Nevada.

Our latest information says the pictures we have of the two bad guys are recent, so we'll recognize them when we get close enough to take a good look. Then there are a number of additional people. We now think there are five, maybe seven more in the network. One for sure has been embedded for four years. The informant, as I told Quint, expired before we could extract all the information in his weak mind. He didn't have much incentive or spirit for the dark side. He was in a field not of his choosing. I believe he wished himself dead. The little he did divulge to us is in the packet."

Jake stood up. "We need more intelligence. Vegas has at least two million souls. How the hell do we find a couple Middle East types in such a large metropolitan area? We are a good team, but this will require a helping hand from the Almighty. Did you, by the way, happen to bring along any good news?"

Sue looked around at the glum faces.

"Yes. I have good news, if you think adding an additional member to the team would be beneficial."

Eyebrows were raised all around the table. They were not enamored with the thought of anyone new joining such an important mission.

Sue said, "Has anyone heard of a Cabal operative referred to as Bernice?"

Jett nodded, Jake and Quint looked at Sue with surprised expressions, but shook their heads.

"Well, since not everyone is familiar with Bernice Pearl, I'll give you an update."

Jake responded, "We had a recent visitor to the shop by that name. She was looking at handguns. She pretended to be a novice, but anyone could see she wasn't. Do you suppose she was checking us out?"

Sue smiled. "You might find her to be one hell of a good partner. She's an expert with the pistol and rifle, and she has black belt degrees in multiple martial arts disciplines. She's one of the few people in our organization who is an Olympic-class shooter with the bow and arrow. Due to her heritage, she thought honing her skills with the bow was a must. She can also dead lift almost 400 pounds. I've seen her take out a 300-pounder, and then lift his dead body to get him out of the way.

"I'm sure you'll be impressed when you get to know her. You've heard the saying about how sneaky Indians are? Well, it's true in her case. Because she's such a small, attractive package, most underestimate her and immediately regret it. Trust me, she will do something to distract you from her beauty and direct your attention to her abilities."

As Sue was finishing her last sentence, the secret door opened slightly. They all jumped up with pistols at the ready. No one could have known about the door, let alone get by the cameras and open it.

The door swung open enough for a hand to slide through holding a white flag. The hand began waving the flag back and forth, and a female voice chanted something in a language no one understood.

Quint remarked, an agitated look on his face, "That must be the topic of our conversation. I would be interested to know how she got into the shop and found the door?"

Jett shouted out to the hand, "You may enter, Miss Pearl. It's time to give us some reason to allow you on our team. So far, all you have done is piss everyone off. We don't need all the drama and sneaking around you have blessed us with."

The hand withdrew and disappeared, and the door slammed shut, muffling the sound of her voice.

Jett suggested to Sue, "You might let your friend know we are getting tired of the antics."

Sue smiled and shot back, "She'll be amongst us shortly, I'm sure."

No sooner had the words left Sue's lips than the grate in the ceiling fell onto the workshop table, with Bernice close behind it, to the surprise of the team, pistols still at the ready.

Jett yelled out, "Good way to get yourself killed, young lady. Blessing your cohorts with a surprise is not in our playbook."

He put the safety back on the .45 and holstered it.

Bernice's first words didn't endear her to Jake. "A blind man could find the secret door, and here I am infiltrating your hidden room through the cooling system. My antics, as you call them, were to show you that I'm not just a pretty face. When you look at me now, you'll see a covert operative of the first order. The rest of the package is a bonus. I've been listening to your meeting from above, and I, too, believe Jett and I could do a lot of good hanging around with the Middle East types. So, if you'll excuse my abrupt entrance, I would like to be accepted as a member of the team. What do you say?"

Sue was smiling, Jake was a little taken aback, Jett seemed to have recovered from his anger, and Quint thought she would fit in just fine. He invited her to join the team. "Have a seat, Bernice. We don't need any more demos."

There were no empty seats, and no one offered her one, so Bernice jumped off the table and dragged up a stool from a work bench near the secret door.

Sue spoke up. "I have a friend in Vegas who has agreed to lease us his digs for as long as need be. The house is located on St. Louis Street in an old neighborhood a couple of blocks from the Strip and the Strat hotel. The house has plenty of room for our needs, and comes with a four-car garage. It's perfect for a safe house and headquarters."

Quint nodded his approval, and said to Jett, "Get the plane ready for departure."

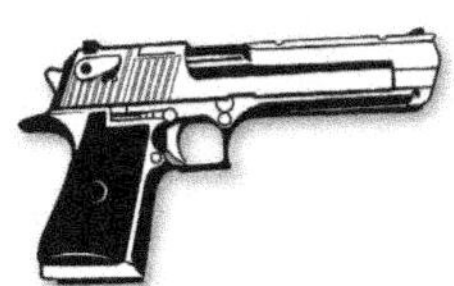

Chapter Five

Yancy Cowcatcher

The weather was perfect when Yancy brought the plane down to the tarmac in what every pilot calls a perfect landing—he didn't crash!

He throttled over to the space he'd used when he picked up the two nerds who had given him cause for a distasteful look into his philosophy of keeping his head clear of all guilt. The small voice that he'd kept hidden in the depths of his soul had been bared. Why those two had triggered his bout of conscience didn't make sense. Why now?

Yancy put those thoughts on hold and idled the plane to a stop, stepped out of the cabin, tied the wings to the rings in the tarmac, and headed for the small terminal. He was hoping to get some information on where the two had come from and when they had arrived in Yuma.

When he entered the terminal, the agent who had assigned his parking spot when he had picked up his charter waved a greeting. "Hello, my friend. Back so soon?"

Yancy got right to the point, not interested in making friends. He pulled a C-note out of his shirt pocket, laid it on the counter, and asked, "Would you happen to know where the two who chartered my plane came from and when?"

The terminal agent just stared at Yancy. He made no move to answer the question, but slid the C-note off the counter and into his vest pocket.

Yancy put another C-note on the counter.

The second note followed the first as the agent's eyes became slits of suspicion. He said, "I do have some information you might be interested in."

The guy could see there might be more green coming his way. Yancy could tell he was stalling around, fishing for more.

He reached across the counter, grabbed the guy by the tie, and pulled him—wide eyed with fear—up close. "I'm losing my patience, friend. The bank is closed. Tell me something to make me believe my money has been well spent."

With the counter no longer a barrier between himself and certain bodily harm, the airport agent decided it was time to drop a dime on his Mexican friends who had smuggled the two charter customers across the border and into Arizona.

"Okay, okay. Jesus, you don't have to assault me. You'll have security over here and create a huge stink."

Yancy eased the agent back over the counter to the floor and released his grip on the tie.

The flustered agent loosened his collar and whispered, "If you want something to find its way across the border in the dark of night or light of day, contact this person." He handed Yancy a business card with only a number on it.

Yancy retorted, "If things don't work out, I'll be back to see you." He walked out of the airport to the curb and waved up a taxi. "Take me to the finest hotel in Old Town."

During the ride to the hotel, he dialed the number represented on the card. After five rings a tired voice answered, *"Hola."*

Yancy answered, *"¿Hablas inglés?"*

The tired voice responded, "If you have something to say, say it."

Yancy didn't like the attitude on the other end of the line, but played along. "I need some information that you're privy to. There is a nice finder's fee, if you give me the info I want."

The cell was silent for a time and then Yancy heard sounds of an argument in the background. It sounded like the guy on the phone was a flunky not high in the hierarchy and had to get orders from the next stooge up the ladder.

A new voice came on the phone. "Shall we speak English?"

Yancy made little effort to keep the annoyance out of his voice. "English is fine."

"My name is Ernesto. How may I assist you, my friend?"

Yancy wasn't used to being everybody's friend. "Well, Ernesto, first of all, I'm not your friend. Second, all we have in common is greed. You have information

I want, and I have the money to buy it. I was told you were the guy to go to."

Ernesto answered, "You are right. You are not my friend, but I assume you have a name."

"My name is Yancy."

"Yancy, what do I know that you don't?"

"If you were responsible for the delivery of two Middle East types to the Yuma airport, I need to know all you know about them."

"So, amigo, how much in Yankee dollars do you think this information is worth to you?"

"Your call, Ernesto."

There was a long pause and more chatter before Ernesto responded, "Five grand each."

Yancy countered, "Twenty-five hundred for both."

"Come on, amigo, you insult me."

"Three thousand for both."

There was another pause on the cell before Ernesto replied, "Five for both."

Yancy smiled to himself, thinking, *These guys are a dime a dozen, and it would be a pleasure to spend my former customer's money to help bring them down.*

"Where can we meet?"

Ernesto paused on the cell again before he answered, "Come across the border into Mexico, first bar on the right."

Yancy smiled again. "No chance, pal. You come to the Yuma airport curb parking in front of the terminal building. I'll be standing in front of Southwest."

"You don't trust me, amigo?"

"No, I don't."

"Okay, gringo, let's meet halfway. There is a small café just inside your border. It's the only one near the border crossing. Shall we say in an hour?"

"Sounds good to me. Be alone, Ernesto."

"You are such a suspicious person, Yancy."

"Let's cut the bullshit, Ernesto. You'd cut my throat for that kind of money, and you're assuming that's not all of my bankroll. The wheels are turning in your fucked-up mind right now, wondering how to clean my clock and take a hike."

Ernesto replied, "I beginning to not like Yancy."

Ernesto said to his gang, "That's the second call today that will help line our pockets. The two dicks we dropped off at the airport called earlier this morning wanting to sell us more drugs. It seems the pilot they hired left them handcuffed to a fuel truck in Nevada and lifted the bag of cash we gave them. Now they need more money. Business is good with these Middle East types.

"The guy who just called was the pilot who flew them to Nevada. He wants to exchange money for information. This is turning into a very lucrative day. We'll meet with the pilot and relieve him of the money he confiscated. We'll have our money back and we'll have the drugs. It doesn't get any better than stealing from someone who just stole something—who they gonna tell?"

Yancy had been about to close his phone, when he heard Ernesto talking to his thugs. The man hadn't punched his cell off, so Yancy was privileged to hear their plans. He returned to the plane and picked up his Colt .45 and .380 before heading to the restaurant. Going to a meeting with a drug smuggling scumbag like Ernesto unarmed would be suicide. He picked up the complimentary vehicle provided by the airport, and drove to the border café.

Yancy parked the car halfway up the street and walked down to the café on the opposite side. He wanted to be there before Ernesto to see how many of his thugs he brought along for the meeting.

It wasn't long before they showed up in two cars. As they piled out, the driver from the lead vehicle directed a couple of guys to cover the back and one to cover the side before he entered the front door.

Yancy waited a couple of minutes, then walked across the street to the side door and took down the hapless gang member. Then, scooting around to the rear, he walked up behind the two others, who were sharing a joint. He put his .45 between the ears of the closest one and ordered them back around to the side, where he gagged them and tied them together. With the opposition out of the way, he entered the front door to find the leader sitting at a table near the rear door.

Yancy, not one to fuck around, walked right up to the table, put the .45 in the man's face, and suggested that he get up and walk out the front door, turn left, and keep walking until further notice.

Ernesto didn't seem intimidated; he just smiled and suggested, "You must be Yancy. You are in deep shit, my friend." He yelled for his backup and smiled again at Yancy. "You gringos are so arrogant and stupid."

When the troops didn't show, his manner became decidedly less foul. "Well, now that we have finally met, how did you know I was Ernesto?"

Yancy didn't suffer fools easily. "You didn't look as dumb as the others out front when you set up the ambush. I just took a guess. Now, move it, senor asshole."

As they walked up the street toward his car, Yancy continued, "Who sponsored my charter people, and what's your connection?"

Before Ernesto could answer, a bullet passed over Yancy's head and a round hit him in the left arm. He whirled around to find the source of the attack.

Ernesto, too fat to run, fell into the gutter, cracking his head on the car bumper.

Diving behind the rear of the car, Yancy crawled around to the street side. He peered over the trunk to see he hadn't tied up the three stooges very well. They were in front of the building on the sidewalk. He was glad they were lousy shots. With the .45 resting on the trunk lid, he pulled the trigger, hitting the new leader in the chest. The others must have figured they were not getting paid to die and fled.

Picking up the dead weight of the unconscious hostage with one arm was a chore. His left arm was painful, but not bleeding too badly because the bullet had passed clean through. He dumped Ernesto in the back seat, slipped behind the wheel, and sped away, hoping to be clear before the cops arrived.

He drove the car up to the plane and rolled the fat drug-dealing smuggler out onto the tarmac. Using the rings meant for planes, he tied him down. Yancy then returned the car and walked back to the plane to find Ernesto awake, but not fully recovered from the bump.

Yancy said, "I have a question for you. If you don't cooperate, I will kill you without hesitation. How you play this will determine your time left here in the real world. I'm sure you don't believe in the virgin shit like your friends. What's your connection with my charter people?"

Ernesto looked around, finally realizing he was not in a position to barter.

"They contacted me with an offer to sell me some drugs dirt cheap and a request to get the two of them across the border. I gave them a quarter of a million for a million dollars' worth of drugs and escorted them across to Arizona."

"Is there a connection now?"

"Yes, someone, who I presume is you, lifted their money and they need more. They called and want me to make another deal. The plan is the same, only I go to Vegas to make the purchase. The amount is the same, a killer deal for the drugs."

"I want to find them, so I'll go to Vegas with you and we'll meet them together, and if things don't go well, you will be the first to die. No matter what happens to me, you're the first loser."

"Why do you care, gringo? Take the money and disappear."

"You know, Ernesto, not long ago that would have been just what I would have done, but things are different today. I'm sure people in your world wouldn't have a clue or give a shit about your country, only using the opportunities it offers for abuse."

The pudgy, short, black-haired vermin with beady eyes retorted, "You, my friend, are soft in the head. Nobody gives a shit unless there is money in it. You can't be that blind or ignorant. Your country is no different than mine when it comes to money. It's all the same. Take the money and go."

"Save the philosophy for our trip to Vegas."

Yancy was thinking, *Shit, I will have my hands on a million in untraceable Yankee dollars, and the little voice is fucking things up.*

Chapter Six

Keno Game

Keno answered his cell. He didn't recognize the number. "Keno here."

Najib stuttered, trying to find the right words. "Pick us up at the front door by eight. Be on time, we have a busy day. You can expect to be on-call all day."

Keno's jaws were as tight as piano wire to keep from reaching through the phone and strangling the arrogant little prick, but he held his tongue and played the obedient driver.

"Yes sir, I'll be out front at the appointed time."

Keno had an hour to get to the hotel, so he decided to cruise over to see a friend at the police substation. He wanted to lift the fingerprints of his fare from the limo and run them through identification, to see if they showed up on any terrorist watch list.

His friend at the substation suggested he pick up his suspects and try to get them to use the glasses provided in the limo, then bring them back to the station. Their prints would be perfect on the glass.

Keno agreed with his friend and headed back to the hotel, hoping to arrive before the two swelled-up assholes came down to the front entrance. He wanted to talk with the doorman and valet parking guys.

He pulled up to the front, and the doorman waved him over to the valet lane and saluted. Keno parked at the curb area provided to pick up guests, leaving the engine running to keep the limo cool. It was still in the hundreds, even in the shade. Actually, he should let them sweat, but then again, he had himself to consider.

The valet parking guy came over and told him that his friends had a single visitor the night before, and he stayed about an hour. He came in the side entrance and left the same way.

Keno thanked the valet and gave him another double sawbuck, to help him stay enthused about keeping his eyes open.

Just as the parking attendant walked away, his clients swaggered out the front door in their usual arrogant manner, brushing people aside and giving them the evil eye.

Keno thought, *Damn, these guys are amateurs in the terrorism business. They should be trying to keep a low profile. But their self-proclaimed superiority doesn't allow them to be humble in any way whatsoever.*

He opened the limo door. "Good morning, gentlemen. Where to?"

Najib handed him a piece of paper with the address of a company on Highland Avenue. "Take us to this address, drop us off, and then wait for my call to pick us up."

Mahathir gave him a dirty look and entered the limo after Najib. It was all Keno could do to keep from slamming the door on the scumbag.

It was the nature of the business for people to feel privileged and high-toned because they were riding in a limo, but these guys took the cake for haughtiness. He might not be able to contain himself if they pushed much harder with their attitude.

He found the address on Highland and dropped them off. Taking note of the business name, Keno pulled around the corner and looked up the phone number. It was an environmental cleaning company for hotel kitchens. He wondered what the hell they would want with such a company.

Keno was cooling his heels at the office when his cell barked. He looked at the number and figured his Middle East friends were ready for pickup. "Keno here."

Najib said only, "We're ready." The cell went dark.

Keno didn't get a chance to confirm the pickup. If things were different, he'd pick those fuckers up, drive them out to Death Valley, and drop them off. The pilot who cuffed them was his hero.

He decided to cut the air off when he arrived at the Highland address and bring the temperature up in the rear of the limo, hoping they would want some water. He had put ice, fresh water, and glasses in the onboard refrigerator.

When he arrived at the building, it was awash with trucks and people changing shifts. He guessed the assault on the bedbugs, roaches, and rodents in the hotels was an around-the-clock battle.

He could see them at the side door waving at him. Keno pretended not to see them with all the confusion and smiled to himself at their frustration, wanting them to be hot and sweaty when they got into the limo. Once it appeared they were about to collapse from all the arm antics, he acknowledged their efforts and steered the limo over to the side door.

When he opened the door for them, Najib was fit to be tied. "Are you blind? It's hot out here and you drag your feet, not paying attention. We are paying you good money to take care of our needs. You will do a better job in the future, or you'll find yourself out of our employ. Do I make myself clear?"

Keno bit his tongue, put his hands in his pockets to keep from bitch slapping the little prick, and replied, "Yes sir, sorry about the mix-up. I was looking for you at the front. All the vehicles during shift change didn't help matters. It won't happen again."

"Good! Now remember we'll be here every day at eight and leave at four. You will be on call twenty-four hours a day."

"I understand, not a problem, sir."

When he pulled away from the building, he looked into the rearview mirror to see them pouring bottled water into the glasses filled with ice. *Bingo!*

Keno dropped them off at the hotel and headed over to his friend at the substation, where he left the glasses, then returned to the office to wait for any news on their prints.

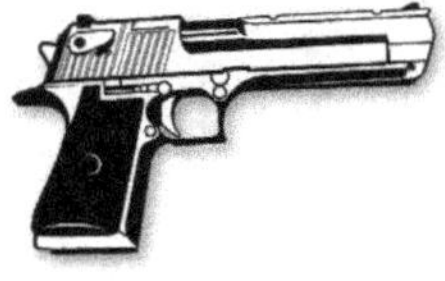

Chapter Seven

Las Vegas

Jett made a perfect takeoff from Bellingham International and dialed in a heading for Henderson Executive Airport, just south of Las Vegas proper. The limited traffic there made it an ideal place to land without any fanfare or prying eyes.

Quint spoke into the headset, "You know, guys, I was thinking. If you wanted information in a place like Vegas, what would be the best way to listen to the talk on the street? I'm thinking what better way than a limo? They go to all the hotels and watering holes where people gather. Anybody who thinks they are somebody uses limos. Using a limo, we would fit right in, not drawing any attention to ourselves while we're on the hunt.

"Sue, the limo driver who took care of me in New Mexico would be a perfect choice. He could get to know other drivers and be in on the street talk, besides providing instant transportation with enough room for us all if need be. It would also give us a good way to haul some weapons around. There are nearly as many limos as there are cabs. We would be invisible right in front of the whole world."

Jett responded first. "I agree, we could always use another hand. What do you know of this guy, aside from driving a limo?"

Sue stepped in. "He's a qualified field agent, with experience in the Middle East and other hot spots. He also has language skills that would be useful. I think he would be an asset."

Quint said, "Sue, would you make the call to have Jesse T. Turbo join us?"

"I'm dialing as we speak."

Sue spoke to her friend, the head of personnel at Cabal headquarters. "Hello Birdie; this is Sue. We are on our way to Las Vegas, and we're in need of an agent named Jesse Thomas Turbo. Would you please have him bring a limo and meet us in Vegas? His field skills, language abilities, and experience in the Middle East will be valuable to our operation."

"Hang on, Sue, I'll check and see if he's available."

The plane was flying over the beautiful state of Oregon when Birdie came back on. "He's on vacation. I'll have to locate him. He may or may not want to join you."

"Birdie, tell him Quint needs him. The last time he drove Quint, he showed an interest in getting his feet back in the field. I think he'll be happy to answer the call."

"Okay, I'll get back to you when I find him."

Sue relayed the information via the headsets and Quint remarked, "No matter where he is, he'll need to go back to headquarters and pick up one of the Cabal's limos. They have special adaptions that aren't available on generic rented limos."

"I'll tell Birdie," Sue replied.

Jett looked over at Jake. "How about flying for a while, Jake?"

Jake, who had been asleep and missed the last hour of the flight, said, "I thought you'd never ask."

He immediately took the plane through its paces, giving everyone an unwanted thrill, thinking the plane would come apart with the unaccustomed stress on the fuselage.

Jett said, "Okay, Jake, let's smooth things out and indulge our passenger's adverse inclination for an early death—by plane."

Quint spoke up again. "Now that the flying circus is over, let's stop over in Reno. We can stretch our legs and make some landline calls. Jesse gave me one of his cards. I might be able to get in touch with him."

Jett responded, "A stopover is already on the flight plan, Quint. But we're going to land in Carson City. We need to fuel up for the last leg, and we're not far out from there now. If you'll look out the port side, that's Lake Tahoe. What a beautiful sight!"

A few minutes after passing over Tahoe, Jake announced that the runways at Carson City airport were in sight.

With a successful landing always a good thing, they throttled over to the designated fueling area. After he deplaned and stretched, Quint walked over to the maintenance shack and used the landline to call Jesse.

After six rings, a groggy voice answered, "What the hell."

"Nice greeting, Jesse. This is Quint."

"Hello, Quint, nice to hear from you. What can I do for you? As you might guess, I had a late night."

"I'm calling to ask if you would be interested in joining a team on a mission of the highest priority in Las Vegas. We need you and one of the Cabal's limousines. Think you might be interested?"

The pause was short. "Hell, yes. If I leave tonight, I can be there in twenty or so hours. Will that fit?"

"Call my number when you arrive. The timing will fit nicely."

When Quint returned to the plane, it was ready for them to continue on to the gambling capital of the world.

Jett made another perfect takeoff, to match Jake's perfect landing, all of which meant they hadn't crashed, as he proudly shared with his passengers.

"It won't be long now. The flight south is only around four hundred miles. That's no hill for a stepper."

The Henderson airport was in the middle of residential housing, having been built when the land was in a desert area, thought to be too far out for any concern. But with the growth in the Vegas valley, the Henderson tarmac was bound by houses on the east and south, the Vegas Strip and I-15 on the west. The main airport, Harry Reid International, was in the center of the city. The huge Nellis Air Force Base was also bounded by homes on the east and south sides, I-15 on the west, and open land to the north. The team had talked about all the possible targets of the terrorists, and it would certainly involve residential neighborhoods if they went after those two airfields.

Jett said, "Take a look, guys. There's the gaming capital of the world. I hope when we leave here, it looks exactly like it does now."

There was a round of agreement.

He made another landing, keeping the rubber side down, and idled over to assigned parking, where the team deplaned once again, ready to begin their hunt for the bad guys.

Quint walked into the terminal building while the others offloaded their gear. He approached the car rental counter to confirm that the crew-cab, one ton pickup he'd ordered was there.

With keys in hand he found the truck and fired it up, turning on the A/C. Even in late August, nearly September, the temperature was in triple digits.

He pulled over to the plane, the team loaded their gear in the back, and off they went to the new digs provided by Sue's friend.

The trip was short in miles but long in time. The traffic was bumper to bumper most of the way until they got to St. Louis Avenue.

"Nice house, Sue. Send our regards to your friend. How much are we paying for the layout?"

"He's a good friend, Quint. What makes you think he's sticking us up for rent?"

"I'm sure he's not donating this pad for old times' sake."

A note of irritation crept into Sue's voice. "Don't worry about it, Quint. If he were out of line with the rent, I'd pay the difference, but that's not the case. He wished us well and wanted to do his part to protect our country."

"Okay! Jesus, Sue, lighten up."

Jake was going over a city map. "We have access to Paradise Road, which runs behind most of the hotels, and the Strip, along with I-15 a few blocks west. There are no major stumbling blocks in our way, just normal traffic. Good choice, Sue."

Quint said, "Let's store our gear and have a serious discussion about where we begin to take down the bad guys."

"Take the money, take the money. You sound like a broken record." Yancy was getting tired of hearing the fucking drug dealer rant about how the money was more important than loyalty to one's country. He thought of throwing the prick out, keeping the money, and taking a hike. But that little voice way down in that never-never land he didn't want to hear from kept tugging.

It was so easy when he didn't give a damn. Now it was a constant tug on his cape. Be the good guy, help your country. Don't let another 9/11 happen if you have a way to stop it. *Jesus, what have I become? A patriot? Shit!*

"Come on, Yancy, you have a greedy character. Admit you would rather have a couple of million than be the good guy. Everyone has their price. What's yours?" asked Ernesto.

Yancy looked over at the cuffed, fat little asshole and retorted, "When I turned over a new leaf, I found a cockroach under it, along with the people you buy drugs from. I think I always knew someday the confrontation of good and evil would come up, and I'd have to decide which side I wanted to die on.

"Well, I've had the showdown. Good won, and you are the guy who will help me square things up. My country has become more important than your blood money. People like you, Ernesto, are lowlife scumbag parasites who live off the misery of others."

Yancy could see the small, out-of-the-way airstrip in Jean, Nevada. Jean was not really a town. No one lived there. But it had a couple of gas stations, a casino, a bucket manufacturer, a prison, and a small fire station. There were plans to build an all-inclusive neighborhood, with a second casino, homes, shopping, and even a hotel. The airstrip was a weekend thing, with little traffic during the week.

He circled a couple of times at high altitude to be sure he was clear of any other aircraft before he made his landing. The parking area was near the modest terminal, where he could rent a car and head for Vegas.

Ernesto was a problem because of the handcuffs. Posing as a deputy sheriff, Yancy dragged the drug dealer through the airport and cuffed him to a tree out front.

"Take the money and leave me. Go back to your airplane and fly out of here. What have you to gain by going through with this insane plan to take down a couple of people from a world away? You're not going to make a difference in the scheme of things. Be realistic, be greedy, be a normal person when hundreds of thousands of dollars are placed right under your nose for the taking. Whoever you hope to take out besides me will be replaced and replaced again. There will be no end. Give it up. Key the cuffs and leave me. I'll find my own way. Take the suitcase and be on your way."

Yancy thought about what the sweaty, fat little pig said for a few seconds. The tug on his cape was powerful. His decision to do something other than feed his greed and ego had been a shock to his system. It was unknown territory he'd not visited in years, but it felt good to be on the right side of things for a change. He'd felt this way on occasion when he first joined the Air Force.

"Button it up, Ernesto, before I put something large and painful in your mouth."

When all the paperwork had been handled at the small terminal, Yancy brought the car around to the front, uncuffed the drug dealer, and recuffed him to the bottom of the front seat on the shotgun side. He'd stopped his whining, not wanting to have a shoe in his mouth.

When they finally got on the road, Yancy asked Ernesto, "Where is your meeting with the drug guys?"

"I'm very uncomfortable bent over like a hunch-back. Take the cuffs off. I'll not give you any trouble."

Yancy had to laugh on that one. "We're never going to be friends, so get used to the idea. Now what's the plan for the meeting?"

"They gave me a number to call when I arrive in the city. That's all I can tell you."

"How much money did you bring in the suitcase to buy the drugs, Ernesto?"

Ernesto replied indignantly, "What the hell do you care, if you're determined to give it up for some silly patriotic notion. You can count it if you want to know. Fuck you!"

Yancy pulled the car over to the side of the road where gravel trucks traveled from their desert pits to town. He parked the car, went around to the passenger door, opened it, and took the cuffs off the drug dealer. He pulled him out of the car, stood him up, and said, "We are going to go at it. You can give it a go or not. In any case, I'm going to pound the fuck out of you."

Yancy was so angry, he was blind. He didn't see Ernesto pull a knife from the inside of his belt buckle. With a long shallow cut across his belly and the blood soaking through his shirt, he found his senses long enough to grab the wrist that held the knife before he could come back across and make another cut.

Ernesto, with the knife immobilized, kicked Yancy between the legs, but missed the intended target, losing his footing. He fell back against the car and down to the ground, jerking his knife hand free.

Yancy had a split second to take advantage of the wingnut and put a foot between his eyes, knocking him out cold.

After he stopped the bleeding from the cut, Yancy tried to arouse the drug dealer, but to no avail. He was dead. The blow had crushed his nose and pushed it up into his brain.

Damn, what the hell do I do now? Shit! I shouldn't have listened to that small voice. I've had nothing but bad luck since. This being a good guy really sucks. What have I got out of this but a headache? Then there is the money in the suitcase and the money that filled the small bag in the plane. Should I head back to the plane, take him up and dump him somewhere in the Mojave desert and take the money like he suggested? Damn this conscience shit!

Yancy searched the body for the phone number to contact the drug dealers and found it in the dead man's inside jacket pocket. It was the only number on him, so Yancy figured it was the right one.

Lifting the heavy body back into the car was a major project because of his stomach wound and arm. The stomach wound started bleeding again.

Yancy decided to go back to the plane, load the stiff, and fly down to the Sea of Cortez, where he would dump his ass out. The body wouldn't be discovered for weeks or months—or never. But first things first. He had to get some stitches in his stomach, and the arm could use some attention.

On the way back to the airport he stopped at the small fire station on the same road. The suitcase sitting on the front seat might be his answer to getting some attention without spreading it outside the station walls.

Yancy parked in the visitor area of the station and propped up Ernesto so it would look like he was asleep, leaning on the window.

He took ten grand out of the suitcase and put it in a brown paper bag, which didn't even put a dent in the stacks of hundreds. He walked into the station, hoping these guys didn't have that little voice tugging at their cape like he did.

While the other fireman on duty watched, the EMT fireman checked out his stomach wounds and then the arm. "Damn, who the hell cut you up? A little deeper and your guts would have fell out. The bullet wound in the arm ain't shit compared to the slice across your midsection. Because of the bullet wound I'll have to report this incident to the sheriff's department. I'm sure you are aware of the procedure. Lie back and I'll stitch and staple you back together."

Yancy set the brown paper bag on the table. "In that bag you'll find some Yankee C-notes. I took the money off the drug dealer who shot and cut me. The money can't be traced. I need for you to keep this incident inside the walls of this station. Patch me up and take the money.

I can't reveal my background, but suffice it to say I have connections to a Special Operations network, investigating terrorists.

So what do you say?"

The other fireman took the bag, walked to the back office, and disappeared. In the meantime the stitches and staples were administered, the bleeding stopped, and his arm was put in a sling.

A few minutes after the wounds were attended to, the fireman returned from the back and said, "I think your wounds were from an accident. I filled out a report for you to sign."

Yancy read the report, put his signature at the bottom, thanked them for their attention, and left the station.

Taking his arm out of the sling, he drove the short distance to the airport. It was now nearly dark and he had an awful task ahead of him: getting the fat-ass SOB into the plane.

He found a two-wheeled luggage dolly and stacked the stiff on it. The short distance over to the plane wasn't a big deal, but getting the late Ernesto up into the plane was a little more difficult. After struggling for thirty minutes, he managed to roll him into the seat, not strapping him in, so he could push him out when the time came.

It was pitch dark when he said *adios amigo* to Ernesto, hoping the body didn't land on some poor fishing boat, when he pushed him out over the Sea of Cortez. The only problem with ditching him was the thought of the drug-dealing scumbag contaminating the pristine waters.

Yancy banked the plane and set a course back to Vegas.

Jesse was happy Quint had invited him to join the team. The chauffeur gig was getting old, and he was looking forward to getting back into the field.

He pulled the limo into the old Highway 66 station in Seligman, Arizona, wishing he'd been around when the old road was the main route across middle America—a time when driving 66 was an adventure for the whole family: theme motels, full-service gas stations, and home-cooked meals in mom-and-pop cafes. Today the freeway system bypassed the heartland scenery and many quaint old towns that were never to be seen again.

Jesse asked the attendant if his full-service station was the last one in the continental United States.

"No sir, there's one in Kingman, Arizona, on the old 66 route there."

He paid the guy and put the past away to visit another time.

As he came up the on ramp to the main highway, there was a BMW on the side of the road. One man was waving for him to stop, while the other was under the hood.

Jesse didn't make a habit of stopping for anything or anyone on the road, but these guys grabbed his attention. They appeared to be of Middle East extraction, and he thought it would be interesting to chat with them and give his language skills some attention.

The BMW indicated they were not vagrants, so he felt reasonably comfortable stopping.

Jesse pulled up behind the stalled vehicle, checked his .380 in case there was a problem, and stepped out of the car. He asked the guy doing the waving, "What seems to be the problem?"

The guy answered in broken English, "The automobile seems to have problem with engine. It stopped. My friend under the hood doesn't know such things. Maybe you help us?"

"Let me take a look."

He walked up to the front of the car and joined the guy looking under the hood. That was the last thing he remembered until he opened his eyes in the back of his limo, tied and gagged.

Jesus, how could you let a couple of dumb fucks take you down so easily? You must be losing your skills. Shit! Be cool and think things through. Analyze the situation and take appropriate action.

Jesse could feel the vibration from the road coming up through the limo floorboard and wondered how long he had been out. Finding himself in such a predicament was his worst nightmare. This was a first for him, and he was steaming for being so lax.

He tried not to move around too much as he wrestled with the duct tape on his wrist. If he could roll over, there was a drawer with a cheese knife and a wine bottle opener for special occasions. The wine glasses were also stored there, and if all else failed, he could break one and cut the tape.

All the thinking and planning proved unnecessary: when he tried to pull his hands apart, the tape crumbled. It must have been lying around for years.

With his hands free, Jesse thought it best to appear that he was still bound until he figured a way to take the two kidnappers out. Unknown to them the speaker system throughout the limo was on, and he could hear them talking in Farsi.

One spoke in a high-pitched voice, sounding almost like a woman, and the other in a deep, low tone, so he named them: High Pitch and Low Tone.

High Pitch spoke rapidly and was hard to understand, but Low Tone was just the opposite. Jesse could understand him easily. He couldn't see them clearly from the floor, but their voices came through the speaker next to the seat above his head. High Pitch was telling his partner how the evil West would fall soon, and they would rule the world.

Jesse's head was beginning to clear as he took an inventory of his predicament and looked around for something to use as a weapon. The only thing in the back were two suitcases on the seat. It seemed that the kidnappers traveled light.

High Pitch was driving, and they weren't paying any attention to the back of the limo. When they slowed down, Jesse pushed himself up to look out and see where the hell they were. He must have been out a long time; the limo was crossing Hoover Dam. While the two were rubbernecking the dam, he opened one of the suitcases to discover it was packed with blocks of heroin.

Damn, these guys have enough smack to make a fortune on the street.

Jesse closed the suitcase and looked around for something to take down High and Low, but there was little in the way of weapons. His only choices were the champagne glasses or the ice bucket.

Once they crossed the dam, the limo sped up. It wouldn't be long before the lights of Sin City would show up. He didn't have much time to decide on a plan of attack. Jesse returned to his tied-up position and tried to remember if there were any hidden compartments in the passenger part of the limo. Before he could have another look, the car slowed and pulled off the main road, climbing and then coming to a stop.

He rolled over to hide his free hands and waited, expecting one of them to open the door and check on him. They must have had some use for him or he'd already be dead. When the door opened, he didn't know which of the two it was, but the man's cell phone rang, and he stopped to answer it. "Yes." There was a long pause. "We will call you back."

He shut the door and returned to the front seat of the car. Jesse could hear them talking about the call.

It was High Pitch who had answered the cell, and he told Low Tone, "That was the Mexican who has the money for the drugs. He wants to meet and do the exchange in the morning."

Low Tone replied, "I'll call Najib. We're almost in town, but we better hang back until we know what he wants us to do. Go back and check on the infidel."

Jesse rolled over onto his hands and hoped High Tone didn't roll him over. He hadn't decided how to get out of the mess yet, but he sensed that this wasn't the right time.

The door opened and a head popped in for a quick glance. High Pitch then slammed the door without getting in.

Jesse rolled back over to look up to the driver's seat. He could hear Low Tone on the cell. "Najib, we have the drugs, and the Mexican called to do the exchange. I told him we'd call him back. The car we bought broke down in Arizona, and we hijacked a limo heading our way. The driver is out cold in the back."

They must have turned on the cell's speaker, because Jesse could hear a new voice.

"Why didn't you kill him? We don't want any loose ends."

"It is our tradition to kidnap and then ransom the infidels."

"You are being very stupid. This isn't the Middle East. Kill him and come to the Strat hotel. Go around to the side door. There's guest self-parking there. Then call me."

Jesse figured it was time to take a hike, so he cut the tape from his feet and as quietly as possible opened the door. He slipped out, shut the door, and ran for the desert, not looking back.

They had parked near an observation point overlooking Lake Mead, so he ran to the wall and over the side. It was steep, with a narrow-gauge railroad track below, a leftover from the dam's construction. It led around the bend towards the dam. He followed the tracks to the old maintenance yard, which was near the highway leading to the dam. From there he caught a ride with a sixteen wheeler heading for a truck stop just off I-15, where a good Samaritan offered him a lift to the Strip.

"He's gone!" yelled High Pitch."

Low Tone answered, "Najib will not be happy. I think we should not tell him about our lax security. We'll make the exchange, give him the money, and be gone. He'll never know we didn't kill the infidel and dump him in the lake."

Chapter Eight

Search

"Najib, we're in the self-parking area behind the hotel. What do we do now?"

"Did you kill the infidel?"

"Yes, he's at the bottom of the big lake. We tied rocks to his feet and dropped him off a cliff. He disappeared quickly."

"Call the Mexican, and tell him to meet you at the Greyhound bus station at the Plaza Hotel. You won't draw any attention carrying suitcases in there. Make the trade and put the cash in one of the depot lockers. Bring the locker key back to the hotel and give it to a limo driver out front named Keno. Ask the doorman to point him out. I'll let him know to expect an envelope. Destroy the cellphones and disappear. You were very stupid to let the infidel live, let alone see you. In the future, if I need any assistance, you two will not be on the list. You're lucky I don't inform your leaders about your stupidity. I'm sure they would have you beheaded. Now, take care of the simple chore with the Mexican and disappear, I don't care how. Just get lost!"

"What do we do with the limousine?"

"Leave the car in the parking lot. Take the license plate off and replace it with one from Nevada. Now go take care of business."

Yancy rented a room at the South Point Hotel. It was on Las Vegas Boulevard, not far from the Henderson Executive Airport.

He was totally exhausted from the previous events, with the bullet hole and knife wound taking their toll. All he wanted was to take a shower and hit the pad for a good night's sleep, but the cellphone rang. It was the Mexican's cell, so the caller could only be the drug dealer.

"Yancy here."

"Bring the money to the bus depot at the Plaza Hotel. We'll be sitting in the depot lobby by the ticket booth with two brown suitcases. Put the money in a locker, then put the key in an envelope and hand the key over. At the same time we'll hand over the cases. We are not alone. There will be others watching our every move."

"No problem. When would you like to make the trade?"

"We'll be there in one hour."

Yancy didn't like the idea of meeting in an hour. The next day would have been lots better. He wasn't up to his A-game, and some sleep would have helped him get back on track.

"Okay, one hour. I'll be carrying a red sports bag. When you see me, stand and wave. I'll wave back, then I'll walk over and put the bag in a locker. Just leave the cases on the seat. I'll pick them up and leave the envelope in their place. If there are people watching out for you, let them know before you show up that if something goes astray you will be the first to die. I, too, will not be alone, so be sure the cases are as advertised. See you in an hour."

Yancy closed the cell. He wished he did have some backup.

Low Tone said, "I think the Mexican is lying about having others with him, but then so are we. There won't be a problem with the exchange. As soon as we drop off the key, we can head back to Canada."

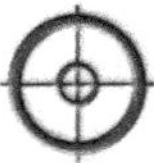

When Yancy walked into the bus depot, he spotted two men sitting with brown suitcases right away. He raised the red bag as they waved in his direction. He stopped, looked around the bus station, and didn't see anything that made him nervous. There were people buying tickets and checking luggage while the usual announcements over the loudpeakers gave notice of buses leaving from different gates. All appeared normal.

He walked over to the dope dealers, said hello, and then proceeded to the wall lockers. He put the bag in the top locker at the end of the row and dropped the key into the envelope he'd brought along. From there he walked back over to the bench area and dropped the envelope on the seat next to the two suitcases. The drug dealers picked it up and headed for the front entrance.

Yancy sat down and opened one of the cases to find the brown papered blocks were as advertised. He picked them up and walked back over to the wall lockers and put them in the locker next to the locker with the red bags. He would stand watch and follow whoever picked up the red bag.

Yancy looked around to find the closest homeless person and offered him a couple of twenties to watch the locker while he took a nap.

The drug dealers sped away, taking the limo back to the hotel's self-parking. With the limo secure, they walked around to the front entrance and asked the swing-shift doorman which limo driver was Keno.

The doorman didn't answer right away, waiting for them to come up with a little something for the information. It took a couple of minutes for them to figure out what the hell was going on and finally give him a fin. He pocketed the money and pointed to the first limo in line.

Low Tone walked up to Keno, who had been leaning on the front fender of his limo watching the doorman pump them successfully.

"This is for Najib." He handed Keno the envelope, turned, and walked away.

Keno took the envelope and watched the two scurry away up the street towards the Sahara. He jumped into the limo to check out the envelope before he called Najib to let him know the delivery had been made. It was a standard white envelope so he just tore it open.

One look inside told him it was a locker key from the Greyhound bus station. He'd been sent to retrieve stuff from there many times over the years. It was as safe as anywhere to hold something anonymously. Number eleven was imprinted on the key.

Najib had told him to expect two men to drop off a package and to call him right away when that happened.

Keno decided to make a quick trip to the bus depot and check out the locker. It would only take a few minutes, and he'd know what the hell was so important. He fired up the limo and headed down Main Street for the short trip to the Plaza. The parking garage's entrance was also the side entrance to the bus depot. He pulled in and stopped in the no-parking zone, as he usually did when he wasn't going to be long.

Jumping out of the limo, he entered the depot's side door. The lockers were straight across from the entrance. Keno walked up to the lockers, found number eleven, and inserted the key. Inside was a large red sports bag. He unzipped it to find neatly packed hundred dollar bills, in good old Yankee currency. Keno figured there had to be in excess of half a million, maybe more.

He zipped the bag up, returned it to the locker, and walked back out to his limo. *Jesus, what the hell was with these guys? Why would they be working at a hotel kitchen cleaning company when they had a huge stash of Yankee greenbacks?*

Keno sat in the limo for a few minutes thinking about taking the bag of money. He would like to see the look on Najib's face when he opened the locker and found it empty.

The homeless guy watching the locker poked Yancy on his bad arm to wake him. *"A guy is opening the locker."*

Yancy sat up and watched the guy open the locker, check out the bag, and put it back. That didn't make any sense. Why not take the bag and be gone? He told the homeless guy to stay put and keep an eye on the locker while he followed the guy out the side door. The man got into a fancy limo, but didn't start it up.

Yancy walked across the garage entrance and hailed the first cab in line. He told the driver to follow the limo in the no-parking zone when he drove off.

They didn't have to wait long before the driver started the limo, made a U-turn, and headed south on Main Street.

The cab driver pulled out onto Main and stayed a couple of cars back from the limo. The trip was short, as the limo turned into the Strat hotel and parked in the passenger pick-up zone. The cab driver followed the signs to the cab lane and got in line.

Yancy gave him a twenty, asking for his business card in case he needed him again. He pocketed the driver's business card and exited the cab quickly. He wanted to be ready to follow the limo driver if he hoofed it.

The front-door area of the hotel was busy, with cars and people clogging the entrance. The doorman was trying to keep an orderly flow, but it was like herding cats. No one was paying any attention to the traffic, be it human or vehicle.

Cooling his heels near the front door, Yancy kept an eye on the limo. The driver just sat there while the other limos were waved up by the doorman.

Keno noticed the cab pulling out behind him from the bus depot. As usual he spent as much time looking at his rear-view mirror as he did looking through the front windshield. The years of driving for high profile clients had often required him to lose or dodge people and cars following his limo. The cab followed him to the Strat and pulled into the cab line.

A big guy got out of the cab, bent over to give the driver his fare, and then walked over to the front door of the hotel, where he stationed himself like a sentry on guard duty.

Keno wondered if he should go right up to the guy and ask him what he found so interesting about him or his limo. After thinking about it, he decided to let things play out. He opened his cell to punch in Najib.

Before he could finish getting Najib on the phone, a drunk opened the rear door, seating himself and yelling for Keno to take him to the closest whorehouse.

Keno stepped out and walked back to the open door. He leaned in and told the guy to get out of the limo, that it wasn't presently for hire.

The guy was an ugly drunk and refused to leave the limo. He said, "You're first in line, and I want a ride. You are obligated by law to take me where I want to go."

Keno reached in and grabbed the belligerent SOB by the neck. Pulling him out of the car was not easy, but on the last tug he threw him across the sidewalk into the wall.

When he bent down to pick him up, three of his friends attacked from the rear. Keno threw the first one over his shoulder and grabbed the second one's arm and threw him to the ground, pouncing on him and rolling over to check for any more assailants. He didn't have to look far, for the third guy was out cold on the sidewalk.

When he got up to finish off the two drunks who were still awake, the hotel security guards intervened, cuffing the four of them. They had thrown them out earlier. The guards told Keno to get back in his limo, the police were on the way pick to up the riotous assholes.

Keno asked the guard, "Who gave me a hand with the ruckus?"

The guard pointed to the big guy by the front door. "That guy put the one on the sidewalk away with one punch to the rib cage. Take your limo for a ride until this mess is cleared up, so you won't be involved with the paperwork."

Keno pulled over to where the big guy was standing and yelled out, "Wanna go for a ride?"

Yancy, surprised by the invitation, replied, "Sure. There are some things I would be interested to know about your stop at the bus depot." He walked up and got in the front seat of the limo. Keno drove around to the back of the hotel for some privacy.

As they drove around to self-parking, Keno noticed a limo that he'd seen come in earlier. The limo had caught his eye because it was dirty, and it had New Mexico plates. Now it had Nevada plates. A good limo driver always kept his vehicle clean and didn't change plates.

He parked a couple of spaces down from the dirty limo, shut the engine down, extended his hand, and introduced himself. "I'm Keno, Keno Game."

Yancy took his hand and replied, "Yancy Cow-catcher."

Keno inquired, "Why did you intervene in the scuffle?"

Yancy didn't respond right away, wondering who this guy was who had walked away from a million bucks. The guy's face looked honest enough, and he didn't appear to be the type to get involved in the drug trade or money laundering, but who knows?

"I would like to say I was just being a good citizen, helping someone who was outnumbered. That, however, is not the case. I didn't want anything to happen to you until I found out why you walked away from a million in Yankee C-notes. Is it your money, or are you a bagman for someone? If you're a bagman, the temptation to take a hike with the cash must have been overwhelming. But then of course you would be marked for death. So, which is it?"

"Yancy, before we get into why I didn't walk with the money, what is your stake in this?"

"Keno, I've been shot, knifed, and gone through a bunch of shit for the last twenty-four hours. I want to know who I'm dealing with—you first. So far I only know a couple of things about you. One, you drive a limo, and two, you are an expert in martial arts."

Keno took a long, hard look at the big guy. He didn't see any evil in his eyes or in his expression.

"Okay, Yancy. It goes like this." He went on to explain his pickup in Sandy Valley, what had transpired since, and how he wanted to keep track of the two in case they were terrorists.

Yancy was surprised to hear that they both had had a hand in the events that brought them together.

"Keno, I'm the pilot who dropped them off in the Valley. Those two are evil." He explained his roller coaster of emotions from trying to let things go to wearing the white hat. He told Keno of his trip to Arizona, dumping the Mexican in the sea, and flying back to Vegas with the money for the drugs. "We have come full circle."

Keno said, "Well, what do we do now? We have a ton of money, a shitload of drugs, and a couple of would-be terrorists. When I give the key to Najib, he'll go to the locker. We could call the cops and let them take him down, but then we wouldn't know if they were the only ones involved."

Yancy suggested, "Let's let things ride for now. Follow the two and see what they're up to. I would take great pleasure spoiling their plans and fast-tracking them to an audience with the Almighty."

"I have to call Najib and see what he wants to do with the key. I'm sure he won't do anything until morning, when I take him and his asshole buddy to their supposed workplace. Why don't you head back to your digs and get some sleep? We can take twelve-hour shifts, you nights and me days. What do you think?"

"Sounds good to me. Maybe we can save the city from an attack. I'll call the cab guy who brought me here. He knows the city and will come in handy when I need to get around."

They shook hands, and Keno drove back around to the front of the hotel, where Yancy got out, hailed his cab, and left for the South Point.

Security had cleared the mess up out front, so Keno took his usual spot in the limo line.

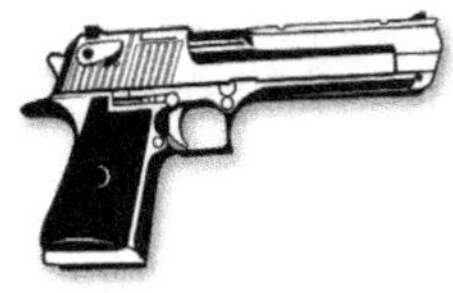

Chapter Nine

Jesse asked the good Samaritan to take him to the Strat hotel.

He hadn't decided whether to call Quint right away, or wait until he found the limo. It would be the height of embarrassment to admit that a skilled, experienced field agent had been taken down by a couple of clowns from the Middle East.

The last words he'd heard in the limo had involved the Strat hotel, so he would begin his search there, where more limos were coming and going than on Oscar night in Hollywood.

He stepped out of the Samaritan's car, thanked him, and waved as he pulled away.

Jesse stood on the sidewalk, looked up, and almost fell over trying to see the restaurant that revolved around the top of the superhigh structure.

Clearing his head, he walked up to the front entrance of the hotel, where people and cars participated in organized mayhem. The display signs indicated check-in only, cab lane, through lane, drop-off lane, valet parking, and directions for self-parking. The scene was directed by the doorman, who looked like an orchestra leader in the middle of a symphony. He was waving vehicles, cabs, and limos forward, and directing guests on foot where to wait for the valet. He kept the situation in fairly good order, considering that half the guests were two sheets to the wind. A whistle between his lips, one hand opening doors, and the other putting the tips in his pocket—the guy was a busy man.

Jesse approached the doorman when there was a lull in the orchestrated mayhem. To get his undivided attention, Jesse approached with a twenty in his hand. "I could use a little information."

The doorman smiled and accepted the twenty, slipping it into his already-bulging coat pocket.

"Go for it. How can I help you?"

Jesse thought, *Damn, maybe I missed my calling. This guy is putting away some serious coin. He took the twenty like it was chump change.*

"Earlier this evening a stretch limo with New Mexico plates and needing a bath, may have come through here. A driver and one passenger."

The doorman thought about it for minute before he replied, "I don't recall a limo fitting that description. I would have noticed a dirty limo and run him off the property. But I'll check with the valet guys and baggage handlers."

"I'm going inside for a beer. I'll check back in a few."

Jesse entered the hotel and headed for the front desk to speak with one of the clerks, but the line was too long, so he found the nearest house phone, which was located by the cashier's cage.

Speaking to the operator, he said, "Would you please page the hotel that a limo with New Mexico plates is blocking the front entrance and will be towed if it isn't moved?"

The operator asked who was requesting the page, and Jesse responded, "I've been sitting in the limo, and the driver has disappeared."

She said, "You'll have to get hotel security or the doorman to request such a page."

"Thank you."

Jesse walked back towards the front entrance, stopping to watch the craps table, twenty-one pit, and roulette. He was amazed at the amount of money changing hands in seconds. *I'm in the wrong business. No knuckles to eat, no bullets to dodge, no explosives to detect, no bad guys on your ass. I might consider retiring to the gaming business.*

When he walked out front, the doorman waved him over. He smiled and stalled around just enough to get Jesse's attention. Jesse put another twenty in his hand. It disappeared as quickly as the first and magically loosened his tongue. "One of the valet guys said you should look around in self-parking. He recalls seeing a dirty limo there when he came to work. If I can do anything else for you, let me know."

He blew his whistle and yelled for a cab to get the hell off the property for cutting in line. The guy ran a tight ship.

Jesse walked around to self-parking to find a huge lot filled to capacity, but it only took a few minutes to find his limo. The New Mexico plates were gone, replaced by Nevada tags.

He decided not to approach the limo, but to stake it out for a while and see if the two kidnappers would return.

While he was waiting, another limo drove by real slow with two guys in it. They stopped for a minute to look at the dirty limo, then continued on and parked a couple of vehicles down. They didn't get out of their car, but sat there talking.

Jesse could see that the two in the limo were not the ones who had waylaid him. After sitting for a few minutes, they drove back the way they'd come.

Jesse waited an hour, and when no one showed, he checked out the limo for damage, walking around it and looking for telltale signs of abuse on the outside. There were none. Checking the inside revealed nothing out of place there either. So far the only thing different was the new plates.

Taking a deep breath and swallowing his hurt ego, he decided to call Quint and confess to being hijacked and kidnapped.

The team members were sitting around the table in the dining room discussing their next move when Quint's cell sang out for attention. He was tempted to ignore the call, but it could be Jesse.

"Quint here."

"Quint, Jesse Turbo."

Quint covered the speaker and said to the others, "It's Jesse, from New Mexico."

"Quint, are you there?"

"Yes. You're coming in loud and clear."

Jesse couldn't get a handle on his voice. It refused to cooperate. He didn't want to reveal his carelessness, how he'd ignored his training and years of experience in the field.

Quint asked, "Well? Cat got your tongue?"

"No, just having a hard time coming up with a good excuse for being carjacked and kidnapped on the way here by a couple of Middle East types. I managed to get the limo back. I'm at the Strat hotel."

He went on to explain the sequence of events, not leaving anything out.

Quint could hear and feel the pain in Jesse's voice. "Not to worry, JT, you have the car back, and we need it. Do you know what they were up to?"

"Not sure about their dealings, but they had a shit-load of heroin. We can dust the limo for prints and see if they have a history. Hang on a moment, Jesse."

Quint held the phone to his chest, turned to the assembled group, and relayed a condensed version of Jesse's ordeal. "What do you guys think?"

Bernice stood up and said, "We can stake out the car and hope they return, so we can find out if they are a terrorist threat or just a couple of bungling thieves with a load of dope looking to replace their broken-down vehicle."

Quint asked for a show of hands. It was unanimous: find out who the guys were.

"Jesse, hang out there and keep a watch on things. One of us will be over to relieve you. Those two could be something to worry about or not. We need to be sure."

"Okay, Quint."

Jesse closed the cell and hoped someone would come over soon. He was ready for a break.

Keno was sitting in line waiting for who knew what, when he decided to take another look at the dirty limo with Nevada plates. He left his limousine at the end of the line and walked around to self-parking.

Standing at the rear of the car he thought it looked a little different from the norm, and it finally dawned on him that the limo was more like one specially built for high-value targets. This was curious, very curious. Why would it be left here. A why were the tags changed?

When he moved up to look in the driver's side window, he felt cold steel behind his right ear.

Keno knew he'd been had, but tried to be cool in a ticklish situation. "Now, my friend, there is no need for the ordnance. I had no intention of stealing this limo. I just wanted to peek inside, because it's a limited edition model. I'm in the limousine business, and it intrigued me."

The gun behind him said, "You couldn't steal it if you wanted to. It's my car, and I'm concerned about two guys who parked it here. You are not one of them. Who the fuck are you?"

Keno figured the guy behind him wasn't an amateur, and the best way to calm him down was to be honest and to the point. "My name is Keno Game. I drive limos for a living. I know who hired the guys who parked this limo here. He's a guest in the hotel, and I was hired to chauffeur for him. If you can put the heater away, maybe we have some common ground here."

Jesse had been burned once already and wasn't excited about having a repeat performance. "I think you have a vivid imagination."

He pushed the button to open the limo and shoved Keno inside, slamming the door and locking it. There was no way to unlock the doors from the inside without a special key. There were some advantages to a specialty vehicle. He'd never figured he'd use the inside-locking device in his lifetime.

He was about to dial up Quint when a car pulled up behind the limo, and a woman jumped out. "Are you Jesse?"

He nodded.

"Good, I'm Bernice Pearl, a member of Quint's team. What do we have here? I saw you push someone inside. Did the kidnappers come back?"

"No. I found this guy snooping around the limo and thought we might want to chat with him in an environment more to our liking. He said he knows the guy who hired the two wingnuts who carjacked me."

Bernice punched in Quint's cell number and explained the situation. She closed the cell and said, "Quint said to leave the limo here and bring him over to the house. I'll hang here and keep an eye on things."

She threw him her car keys.

Jesse opened the limo. Holding the pistol on his prisoner, he said, "Get out, turn around, and face the door. We can do this the hard way or the easy way. You, my friend, are involved in some serious shit here, and I won't be making any miscalculations on your intentions. Do I need to cuff you?"

"Look, pal, I was just trying to figure out what the hell was going on, same as you. I picked two Middle East types up in a valley not far from here, and things have snowballed ever since. I'm on your side, no need for the cuffs. I'm more than willing to help you figure this out."

"Okay, get in the car. We're heading over to a safe house nearby to have a chat with the others involved in getting to the bottom of this convoluted mess."

Jesse turned to Bernice. "One problem, Bernice. I don't know the address of the safe house."

She was on her cell and closed it to answer Jesse. "That was Quint. He said to stay put. The others are on their way here. Your guy there might have stumbled onto the people we're looking for."

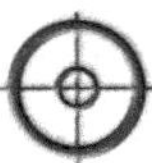

Keno, after hearing the conversation, decided he really had stepped into some serious shit. If he'd just driven the limo and minded his own business, there wouldn't be a gun in his face or reinforcements on the way.

Keno asked Bernice, "Who the hell are you guys? I don't see any badges. Who are you, to detain me?"

Bernice answered, "We work for a private company looking into a terrorist threat in Vegas. You may be the guy who'll lead us to the scumbags. Actually, we can't hold you, but you did appear to be trying to steal the limo. Jesse was just trying to keep his car from being taken again. If you want to give us a hand, we would appreciate it."

Keno retorted, "I need to know more about your private company and you people before I commit to helping you. For all I know, you're here to knock off one of the casinos."

Bernice returned to her car to retrieve the pictures they had of the terrorists. She presented them to Keno. "Do the two guys that hired your limo look anything like these two?"

Keno took a long look at the pictures and said, "Yes, those two are the guys I picked up in Sandy Valley and brought to the hotel, as I was trying to tell your friend while he was holding a gun to my head. I believe you are on the right trail. These guys are arrogant SOBs, up to no good. Okay! How can I help? Oh! By the way, I met the pilot who flew them in from Arizona. He has quite a tale to tell about those two."

Bernice thought they might have hit the mother lode, if this limo driver and his new friend were telling the truth. "How can we get in touch with the pilot?" she asked.

"He's staying at the South Point Hotel. His name is Yancy Cowcatcher."

Quint, Jett, and Jake pulled into the Strat's self-parking to find Bernice, Jesse, and the limo driver standing behind Jesse's limo.

When they'd all gathered in a circle, Bernice introduced everyone and said, "Keno knows the guy who flew our friends in from Arizona."

Keno shared the events leading up to the present, including his experience at the bus depot lockers and the story of how he met Yancy, the pilot. He explained why they thought the two guys might be dangerous and why they wanted to keep tabs on them.

When Keno had finished, Quint said, "Well, Keno, welcome aboard. Bernice said you made a positive ID that the guys you brought to the hotel were the ones in the pictures. They are indeed the bad guys we are looking for. When do you expect them to call for you?"

Keno answered, "In the morning, around six."

"Good. Maybe we can wrap this up in the morning. Now let's find Yancy. Keno, can you take Bernice in your limo to the South Point, where Yancy's staying?"

Bernice's thoughts began to wander to past times as Keno steered the limo down the Strip towards the South Point Hotel.

Five years had passed since she'd taken a contract to eliminate a Somali assassin who had finally made a mistake and left a crack in his modus operandi.

The Cabal told her the mission would require a high altitude, low opening parachute insertion on the outskirts of Mogadishu in the dead of night. Her HALO drop zone would put her in position to hijack a vehicle driven by a woman who regularly performed a special sex act upon her target. The woman would be driving to the target's safe house, where she appeared once a week. Her visits were so regular that the car was not stopped and searched, but waved through by the security guards posted around the area.

The target was a sadist and a masochist. The woman was a specialist in the art of torture, bringing her customer near death before providing relief.

Bernice could see it like it was yesterday. She could relive the freezing cold as she jumped out into the thin air, bearing weapons, air tanks, masks, and all the gadgets to keep her on course and alive from the lofty heights to the open field that she hoped to hit on target. There was little room for error in her low opening landing.

As it was with all well-laid plans, the hair-raising company of Murphy was always a threat. She landed in a tree, not the flat, soft area on the map. SNAFU was the norm. Luckily she was hanging heads up. It didn't take long to cut away all the equipment and drop to the ground only a few minutes behind schedule.

Running to her position near the road, Bernice pulled her jumpsuit down to expose the dress she had donned for the evening's event. She would flag down her mark, pretending to be in distress. The small caliber pistol, knife, and garrote concealed under her dress were her weapons of choice.

She could see the lights of a vehicle coming up the road a half mile from the target's house, which sat upon a small rise. The view from the house gave the occupants a heads-up to any visitors. The approaching car was right on time, and she hoped it was the right vehicle for her charade.

When the lights were close enough to see her, she stepped into the middle of the road, waving her arms as a sign of distress.

The car skidded to a stop about ten feet from hitting her. The veiled driver rolled down the window and yelled something unintelligible, waving her arms to clear the road.

Bernice ran toward the car, yelling, "Help, please help me!"

The woman in the car rolled up the window, and then killed the engine trying to take off. Bernice shattered the driver's window and reaching in, grabbed the cellphone the woman was trying to use, and knocked her out cold with one hit to the temple, using the butt of her handgun.

She dragged the domination freak out of the car, laying her down near the trunk. After exchanging outer clothing with her, Bernice stuffed her into the trunk.

Jumping into the car, she fired it up, cleaned up the broken glass, and rolled the window all the way down to conceal the damage. She continued up the road, hoping the delay wouldn't cause any of the guards to question her or search the vehicle.

As she approached the guard shack, the barrier was raised and they waved her through, giving her that knowing look of approval. The guards were wishing they were the ones to be with her instead of their boss. Little did they know of the weird appetite she was about to bring to an end.

She skidded to a stop and ran up to the door of the house and knocked, hoping there wasn't a special code between her target and the dominatrix in the trunk.

On the third rap, the door swung open and a huge man filled the doorway. He was saying something she didn't understand, and just as she was about to take a quick exit, he stepped aside to reveal a skinny, naked man waving for her to enter.

Thankfully, the veil she had stripped off the woman covered her face. With her straight black hair and her brown-hued skin, she could pass as a double for the other woman. The charade could continue until she had an opportunity to take the scrawny little fucker out.

The target directed her to the back bedroom of the house and followed her in. She turned just as the door slammed shut, relieved that the big guy hadn't followed them into the room.

The bag of bones pushed her towards the bed, handing her a whip he'd picked up from the chair by the door. He yelled at her in a language she didn't understand. When she didn't respond to his words, he reached out and pulled her veil off, which gave her the opportunity to stick him in the heart with her knife. He gasped once, grabbing her as he slid down to his knees, jerking, the blood flowing from his wound and mouth. He kept clutching her, so she pulled the garrote out and looped it around his neck to finish him off.

The body was light. She easily lifted the stiff up to the bed, wrapping it in the comforter. Turning the rug over to cover the blood, she yelled for the bodyguard in the basic Somali she had learned before deploying on the mission. Figuring he was used to the screaming, she opened the door and waved for him to enter.

He hesitated at first, not sure of the invitation. Finally he stepped into the bedroom.

Bernice pointed to the bed. When the bodyguard bent over the bed to get a closer look, she put the .380 to his temple. It was loud, but then, noise coming from the house when the woman was visiting was not unusual.

The big guy dropped like a rock, crumpling to the floor in a heap. With her weight training, she rolled him over with ease, searched him, and relieved him of his weapons, ID, and money. There was a metal ring in his pocket with cars keys she thought might come in handy if she had to switch vehicles. She picked up the veil before she left the room.

Bernice sat in the living room, wondering how long to wait before leaving. There hadn't been any information on the dominatrix's performance time. Sitting with the two stiff assassins was a little creepy, but then again, she'd done the world a favor.

After an hour she peeked out the window, and not finding anything unusual, she put the veil back on. Opening the front door, she slipped back into the dead woman's car. Turning around she headed for the gate that she'd come through on her arrival, hoping once again they would pay her no mind.

When the barrier wasn't raised, she had to come to a complete stop. A guard with an ugly, toothless grin walked up to the driver's side and put his hand on her shoulder, saying something she didn't understand. She got the idea as he tried to move his hand down her front.

Looking around for the other guard, she yelled for help, but no one responded. She grabbed the knife hidden in the sheath on her leg and stuck it in the toothless guard's throat with enough force that he fell away from the car.

Jerking the knife out as he fell, she opened the door and ran to the guard shack. The other guard had been asleep on the floor, but she'd made too much noise, and the grimy, smelly sentry jumped up. He was so startled that in his panic he fired his rifle wildly.

Bernice slammed her pistol into his face, knocking him down with a crushed nose and cheek bone. While he was down and out, she cuffed and gagged him. It was only when she started out the guard shack door that the pain in her left arm got her attention. In all the excitement she hadn't felt the bullet go through her arm. It left a nice clean hole that was beginning to bleed profusely.

Wrapping the wound with the veil from her costume, Bernice jumped into the car and headed down the road, hoping to find the beach for her escape before the discovery of the dead at the assassin's compound. She had to get to the small pier in the dark, where the fishing boat would pick her up and take her to Mombasa, Kenya and a private flight to Nairobi, where she would catch a commercial flight home. She ditched the car and costume a half mile from the beach and found the pier without much trouble. The boat was waiting.

"Bernice, Bernice, we're here. Hello, where are you?"

She could hear Keno's voice, but couldn't figure out where the hell she was. It took a minute to clear her head and find her way back to the real world. The sweat was running down her face, as the past slipped away to wherever it goes. She said, "I'm okay. Just had a short trip into the past. I haven't had much sleep lately. Guess I should do something about that. Short naps aren't doing me any good."

Keno said, "I'll check at the front desk if you want to wait in the car." He looked at her with concern. The woman was sweating bullets and appeared to be physically ill. "Are you all right?"

"Yes, thank you. I'll be fine. That short trip into a past assignment brought back memories that should be left untouched. I'll wait in the limo."

Keno had his doubts about the woman, but if she was part of the group looking for the terrorists, then she must be a pro.

The desk clerk at the South Point wouldn't give out any information on a guest, even with a little greenback incentive. So Keno suggested to the clerk that he call the room and tell the occupant that a man named Keno wanted to talk to him.

"Hello, Keno. What's up? You didn't leave me much time to rest up."

"We've stumbled on what appears to be a major terrorist plot, and the people who are here to thwart the event would like your assistance. I've already thrown in with them. If you'll come down to the lobby, I'll introduce you to one of the team members. I think we can help."

Bernice, still coming out of her fog, saw Keno and a huge guy coming out the front door of the hotel. The big guy was walking with a limp, and his left shoulder was leaning lower than the right. He didn't look happy.

Keno opened the front door and introduced Yancy to Bernice, "Yancy, Bernice Pearl. She'll fill you in on what's going on. I'll drive the limo back to the safe house."

"Hello, Yancy. From what I've heard, you could help us a great deal and would be a welcome member of the team. Let's get in the back, and I'll explain the team's mission on the way to the safe house." Yancy already had a lot invested, so she didn't have to say much to get him recruited as the newest team member.

After he agreed to join, Bernice said, "Let's wait until the whole team is present before you tell us about your time with the bad guys. It will be a major piece of the puzzle."

After introductions all around, Yancy relived his experiences with the two Middle East wingnuts and the puke Mexican drug dealer. Between himself and Keno there was enough factual information to take down the two would-be terrorists and their contact.

Quint was the first to speak. "This couldn't be any better. So far Murphy's evidently sitting on the sidelines for this one. We have positive ID on our targets, their location, and some of their itinerary. How good can it get? All we have to do is act."

Jett jumped in. "Let's not be hasty. Let Keno take them to the kitchen-cleaning place, and when they're at work, we'll check out the company they are employed by. We want to be sure they are the only ones involved. If they are, Keno can take them for a ride into the desert and add them to the stiffs the mob left out there—all people who got greedy. A job well done. Case closed."

Jake and Bernice chimed in at the same time. "This is too easy."

Jake allowed Bernice to speak. "Murphy is not dead. Except for Yancy's adventure, this has been way too simple. Something is wrong with this picture right now—or will be. We haven't even had time for piss-poor planning. I suggest we step back a little and go over again what we have and how we got it."

Quint responded, "Okay, let's start from the top. Keno, do the two guys go to the same hotel everyday with the cleaning company?"

"No, I've followed them to a different hotel each day, but I don't see either of them doing any manual labor; they are way too arrogant for that. I think they are using their positions to recon the hotels as potential targets. That makes me think their foreman is being paid to let them wander through the hotels, or he's in on whatever plot is in the making."

"One more thing, Keno, do we have anyone shadowing the duo?"

Keno smiled and said, "Yes, the bell department is watching their rooms, and the valet guys are watching the front and rear parking, including all the pickup areas for tours and such."

Quint nodded his approval and remarked, "With our six covered for the night, let's all get what sleep we can. In the morning we'll do some serious planning to take down the wannabe terrorists."

Chapter Ten

The Search

Najib put the phone down and turned to Mahathir. "We are going to change our base of operation. Mohammed thinks the hotel staff is paying too much attention to us. He also suggested we fire the limo driver, and he has changed our work from the kitchen patrol place to Citywide Mechanical. We'll have access to the roofs and ventilation systems of all the major hotels.

"He's going to pick us up before dawn, so we can disappear in this city of two million. The sound of crumbling buildings will be the death toll for thousands. The infidels will hear from us, but it will be too late for them. They will die by the thousands, and we'll be on our way to paradise."

"Murphy has rained on our parade!" Quint's voice could be heard throughout the house. "Keno just got a call from the valet parking guys at the hotel. Our pigeons have flown the coop. He saw them jump into a black SUV, but didn't get the plate number."

Quint's loud voice had awakened everyone, and they now gathered in the living room, expecting to hear more details—but there were none. The three terrorists had gotten away and would have to be hunted down, with little to go on.

Jet stood and said, "I wonder what spooked them?"

Keno said, "Probably the third guy, who must have been watching his companions and noticed the subtle attention the hotel staff was paying to his friends. It won't be easy to find them now."

"Piss-poor performance on our part," reflected Bernice. "One of us should have stayed at the hotel."

Quint said, "Look, it's spilt milk now, so let's get our act together and get started. First things first. Yancy and Bernice, you head out into the city's hookah shops and see if you can listen to the local gossip and find something. Sue, you and Keno start cruising the Strip and check out the hotels. Keno knows all the door-men, valet parking guys, and bellmen. They would have a good chance of seeing our Saudis. They will have to hole up somewhere. Flash the pictures we have and see what shakes out.

"Jake and Jett, you guys head over to the kitchen-cleaning place where they were working. Since they took a hike, I doubt if they're still around, but you never know. There is a difference between clever and smart.

"I'm heading over to the hotel to go through their rooms with a fine-tooth comb. It could be they over-looked something. Okay, let's hit the bricks!"

Yancy looked at Bernice as she thumbed through the Clark County phone book, wondering what possessed a woman to get involved in such a dangerous business. She looked like the girl next door, but her position in the black-ops world belied any similarities. Trying not to get caught staring as she looked up when she felt his eyes on her, he said, "Well, how many hookah bars are there?"

"They're all over town. So I suppose we'll start here east of the Strip."

Bernice, riding shotgun, kept track of the building numbers as they traveled down Paradise Road, heading south. She said, "I think the address we're looking for is at the south end of Paradise between Flamingo and Tropicana."

Yancy kept the car in the middle lane, waiting for Bernice to direct him right or left. He remarked, "The last time I drove down this street the convention center looked like a spaceship and the Landmark Hotel was still on the corner. Damn! How things have changed over the years. I bet the long-time locals don't care so much for the influx of people, buildings, roads, and pollution in their small valley."

Bernice was only half listening while checking out the street numbers, when she shot back, "Left here, Yancy!"

They pulled into a shopping mall with parking in front of each small business. The hookah bar was in the middle between a sandwich shop and a bottled water sales place. The parking lot was nearly full, which was a good thing for them. They wouldn't stand out in the crowd.

Yancy pulled into the only vacant space near the bar. Before shutting off the car he suggested, "We might leave the car unlocked in case we have to vamoose in a hurry." Bernice nodded her approval. They exited the car and walked down to the bar's entrance.

Yancy pulled the door open and held it for Bernice as they entered. The place was nearly empty, with just four patrons sitting at a table using the community hookah water pipe. There was a heavy odor of fruit in the air. The table of four looked over at the door as they entered, then went back to their quiet chatting, seemingly not paying much attention to the newcomers.

The proprietor of the establishment, wearing a white apron, waved them a greeting and guided them to a table near the front window. He handed them a menu. "What would you like to drink?"

Yancy said, "We would like some water and a small salad."

The apron suggested, "Bottled water would be the best choice. The tap water here is not good. And would you like to use the hookah?"

"No, the hookah won't be necessary. The lady and I are in a bit of a hurry. The salad and bottled water will be fine."

When they were alone, Bernice looked over at the table of four and lowered her voice. "Those guys don't seem pleased to see unfamiliar faces in their neighborhood. I wonder if it's because a woman has invaded their space or if they just don't like strangers?"

The proprietor delivered the bottled water and casually remarked, "You're not from these parts are you. I don't recall seeing you in here before."

Bernice answered, "We were checking out the Strip and off-Strip hotels and decided to have lunch. And here we are. We're from California."

The waiter wasn't impressed with the coy answer, and as he turned, he peered over to the table of four and shrugged his shoulders.

Yancy remarked, "I think these Middle East types are paranoid. Suspicion is their middle name. It must suck to be them." He continued, "I don't think they're melting into the melting pot. I think they are bringing with them the very reasons for which they immigrated. This multiculturism may not be such a hot idea. The language barrier is only one of the real threats to peaceful communication."

"You're a pilot, Yancy. What do you do if you have an emergency and have to land at a large international airport? You call in your emergency to the tower and request landing instructions. The guy in the tower is a product of multiculturism, so he only speaks his native language, and it isn't English. What would you do?" asked Bernice.

"That's a no-brainer. All pilots and towers around the world speak English."

Bernice responded, "That's the point. If a country wants a peaceful society, they need to communicate. The best way for the citizens to get along and understand each other is to speak the same language.

In France they speak French, in Germany they speak German—you get the point.

"The foundation for a peaceful nation is a common language among the people. Communication is the key."

"Bernice, what the hell has all that got to do with our search? These guys probably speak their native language and English. As a matter of fact they are speaking in their native language right now, and there're not happy with two strangers invading their space."

"I can't hear them from here. Do you have bionic hearing or what?"

Yancy smiled. "I read lips, and they would rather we were gone. So let's oblige their wishes. We're finished with lunch. Let's take a powder. These guys may be nervous, but they are not a threat. Just prejudiced against women and strangers. Old habits from wherever they came from."

"Okay, Yancy, let's go."

Bernice gave the four at the table a hard look, and waved at the proprietor for the lunch check.

He brought the check over with a sort of smirk, rather than a thank-you smile, and dropped it on the table, giving every indication their patronage was not on the top of his list.

Yancy paid the tab, left a generous gratuity, and they departed the hookah bar.

After they got outside, Bernice said, "What the hell! Why did you leave so much on the table?"

"We may come back here sometime, and money talks. The proprietor might be loyal to his friends to a point, but he has to make a living and that comes first. I'm sure his display of indifference was for the benefit of his table of four. If those guys hadn't been there, I'm sure he would have been more amicable. Where's the next stop?"

The Strip was crowded as Sue and Keno left the safe house. "Let's start at the south end of the Strip and work our way back down town," suggested Keno. "We'll stop first at the Mandalay Bay. Not much more that way except the South Point, and we've been there already. We can tack back and forth from the east side to the west side and hit all the hotels heading back.

"I know most of the doormen and with a little incentive, they will be more than happy to give us a hand. A C-note will boost their observation skills and memory capabilities. We better stop and stock up on hundred-dollar bills. Lots of hotels on the Strip, and that's just the beginning."

As Quint strolled up to the bell desk at the Strat, he reached into his pocket for some cash to perk up the bell captain, who greeted him with a handshake. "Hello, Mr. Michaels." A C-note was transferred between the two, invisible to those not paying close attention. Quint said, "I would like to have a look at the rooms our Middle East types vacated last night."

"Not a problem, I'll walk you up there myself," answered the captain. "Do you think there is something in the room the housekeepers may have overlooked?"

"No. I'm sure they cleaned the rooms in their usual professional manner, but there is always something left behind. It may be too small to draw any attention to someone who isn't necessarily looking for the unusual."

The bell captain led the way to the service elevator and pushed the ninth-floor button. It stopped on the seventh floor, where a couple of maids joined them, pushing their cleaning carts full of linens and equipment aboard. The doors closed as the crowded elevator continued up to the ninth floor, where Quincy and the captain exited and headed down the hall to room 909.

The captain, using his master key, led them into the recently-cleaned room. The connecting door to 911 was still open, as the maids were just finishing up their cleaning. The captain waved and said, "It's okay; we are just checking rooms."

The maids were not happy with the captain, figuring he was spying on them and pushing to get the rooms cleaned quicker. They already thought they were doing too many rooms and didn't need any assistance from the high-toned bell captain.

The captain remarked, "Doesn't look like there is anything to be found here!"

Quint replied, "Well, I'll have a look around. Thanks for giving me a hand. If I need any further assistance I'll give you a call."

The captain beamed, thinking about adding another hundred to his collection. He shot back, "Anything for you, my friend," as he stepped into the hall, heading back to his post at the bell desk.

Quint surveyed the room. *Damn, the bell captain may be right about not finding anything of value in the rooms!*

He looked around room 909 first and found nothing of interest. Moving through the connecting door to room 911, he again checked the obvious places like the bathroom and the living room couches, hoping to find something that had fallen in between the cracks from someone's pocket.

The closets were clean as a whistle. Finding nothing out of place or unusual, his last hope was under the king-sized bed. He moved over to the bed, knelt down, pulled the comforter up, and peered under it. He was about to drop the comforter when his eyes caught sight of a small piece of paper near the headboard. Reaching the length of his arm, he grabbed what was left of a matchbook. Standing up, Quint walked over to the window for more light, hoping to find some advertisement that could be read from the small piece.

To his surprise, there were four letters legible on the torn cover. He could make out the letters *"ver D"*. As he read the letters, an idea came to him. He opened the door, checking the hallway for a maid. Seeing none, he walked down the hall to the maids' station, where he found them taking a break. He asked, *"¿Hablas inglés?* The youngest in the group stood and said, *"Sí,* I speak okay English."

Quint reached into his pocket and withdrew a double sawbuck. "I want to borrow the vacuum used to clean rooms 909 and 911. Take the twenty and give me the vacuum for half an hour or so."

The young maid was not sure what to do, but she didn't want to turn down the twenty. She didn't have to make the decision. An older maid who understood more than she had been willing to admit gave up the vacuum and snatched the twenty from Quint's hand.

Quint accepted the vacuum and walked back to room 911. He took the bag off and dumped the contents into the bathtub. He was amazed at the amount and size of junk it could pick up. Taking great care, he found the rest of the matchbook, and with way more patience than he would have thought he possessed, he fitted the torn pieces together.

The end result of the puzzle was a matchbook from the Boulder Dam Lodge near Hoover Dam. *Damn, these guys are thinking big time, if the dam is one of their targets!*

Gathering up the debris from the tub, Quint returned it to the bag, put everything back in order, and walked the vacuum back to the maids' station. The maids were further down the hall cleaning another room. He stopped, gave the vacuum to the young one, put two twenties in her hand, smirked at the older one, and continued down the hall to the elevator. The older maid gave him a look that could freeze the Mojave Desert.

Jett looked over at Jake. "Do you think they'll be honest with us about our terrorist suspects?" he asked, as they pulled up to the front office of the cleaning business.

"No. If they think there is something illegal going on with them, they'll cover their ass."

Scratching his head, Jett said, "Guess we'll find out soon enough."

They parked the car and entered the front door, stopping at the information desk. The cute little receptionist was pleasant but apprehensive as Jett said, "We are here to see the manager," in a rather gruff voice.

The young lady was a little tongue-tied at the sight of the two big men as she pressed the intercom. "Two gentlemen to see you, sir." There was no answer, but a door opened behind the receptionist, and a man walked out. The mirror on the wall must have been one of those I-can-see-you-but-you-can't-see-me deals. It was probably a good thing for the manager to know who wanted to see him if the kind of help he hired was generally like the ones the team was looking for.

"Hello, gentlemen; how may I help you?"

Jake produced a phony private investigator's ID and Jett showed the weary manager pictures of their quarry. "Do you know these guys? And if you do, where are they?"

"Yes, I know them, and I don't give a fuck where they are, as long as they are not here."

"Look, man," Jake said, "we need to find them ASAP."

The manager, not sure if he was talking with the real McCoy or a couple of loan sharks trying to collect a debt, shot back, "I remember them talking about air conditioning yesterday, but I didn't pay any attention at the time. The only reason I hired them was the recommendation of their friend, Al Mormar."

Jett asked, "Do you have a photo of this Al guy?"

"Sure." He turned to the receptionist, who could feel the tension in the air. "Get the personnel file on Al Momar."

She retrieved a folder and asked, "Do I put him in the not hireable file when you're finished?"

"Yes."

He handed the photo from the file to Jett. "He was okay until the other two showed up, and from then on the three of them were worthless as a parachute on a ship. I hope you find them and they get their just reward."

Jett thanked the manager for his assistance. "Okay pal, you've been a lot of help. The picture of Al Momar is very important. If you hear anything from those three, give us a shout." He handed the manager a card with his cell number on it.

The manager said, "No problem, you'll be the first to know."

Jake followed Jett as they retreated out of the building, to the obvious relief of the receptionist, and headed back to the safe house to report their good fortune of acquiring a photo of the third guy.

Sue remarked, "Well, that's every hotel on the east side of the Strip, and we've come up with zip. You want to head back to the safe house and check on the west side this evening?"

Keno answered, "I think we should finish the west side first. It won't take that long, and the earlier we get the word out the better. Let's start at the Circus Circus."

"Why there?"

"We've been to the Strat, and they're next. Good place to find a couple of clowns."

"Very funny. I wish we were dealing with a couple of clowns, instead of a serious threat to the city and the country. Who knows, maybe we'll get lucky and find these guys before they head for the happy hunting grounds and take a hotel with them. They win every time when they commit suicide as a tool for murder."

After checking with the doormen at most of the hotels on the west side of the Strip, they returned to their temporary headquarters, empty handed, hoping that someone else had discovered something. They prayed the hundred C-notes they left around as an incentive for the hotel people to keep their eyes and ears open would bear some fruit.

When they got back to HQ, everyone was present except Yancy and Bernice. They were cheered by the good news about the picture of Al Momar.

Quint said, "We'll give them a little more time to return before we panic. Bernice is usually very prompt. I think they were heading for the other side of town after their first stop on Paradise. Maybe they found something and had to do a little more investigating. We can wait for a while. It's important that everyone hears each others' reports."

The last thing Yancy remembered was seeing the look of surprise on Bernice's face as the blackness overtook him.

Lying on the floor trying to remember what the fuck happened, he discovered his hands and feet were bound with plastic zip ties.

Shaking his head, Yancy tried to clear the cobwebs. Looking around he discovered Bernice lying next to him, with a blood-soaked rag around her head. She wasn't moving, but he could hear her breathing. Yancy was relieved to know she was alive. She was bound as he was, hand and foot with zip ties.

He rolled over and whispered in her ear, "Bernice, are you with us?"

She moaned and her lips moved, but not enough to read them and no sounds were forthcoming. On her second effort she spoke just loud enough for Yancy to hear. "I believe we really pissed someone off. Being blindsided is not a lot of fun."

Yancy scooted around so they were face to face. "I know. I didn't see the attackers."

Bernice shot back with swollen lips, "I saw them waylay you, just before I was hit in the head from behind, but the blow didn't put me down. I managed a knife hand to the throat of the closest one to me. He died with a broken windpipe. The other one, I put two fingers in his eyes, and he was on his way to the happy hunting grounds. He bled out in minutes, because I have little razor blades glued underneath my nails. They couldn't call anyone to save him and explain the situation without causing one big FUBAR. I see the two stiffs are lying across the room there. The second blow put me out. So, here we are!"

Yancy hadn't noticed the two bodies across the room. Now he looked at them and thought, *Bernice must be as advertised. Nice that she's on the side of the guys who wear the white hats.* He said, "Well, you're the expert, what do we do now?"

"I guess for now we can just lie here and heal up a little, hoping they don't come back and finish the job. If we were in their country they would have filmed our beheading. Brave souls these assholes are not. Toe to toe they are cowards who will never get out of the tenth century. It looks like we're in the kitchen area of the hookah bar."

Yancy remarked, "I don't suppose you have a magic trick to let our pals know our situation?"

As Bernice was about to share her brilliance, two of the bad guys came into the room. They were exercised about something, with a heated argument going on between them. After a lot of arm waving and yelling they left the kitchen.

"Okay, Yancy, it's your turn to contribute to our present situation. What the hell were they arguing about?"

"Bernice, I think we're dealing with a couple of amateurs. They don't know what to do with us. One of the guys you killed was a hard-core operative who happened to be in the bar when we arrived. He talked them into capturing us to use for propaganda. These two have melted into the American dream and have little sympathy for their old country. They are simple businessmen who made a hasty, wrong-headed decision to please the hard-core guy you dusted.

Maybe we can negotiate with them. When they come back, we'll offer them a way to dispose of the stiffs without a trace and agree not to make an issue of our being kidnapped."

"If you're right and they don't have a clue what to do with us or the bodies, they might just agree to back up and cover their ass. The two who are dead can't tell anybody from their world what happened. I think they would be more than happy to put this episode behind them," replied Bernice.

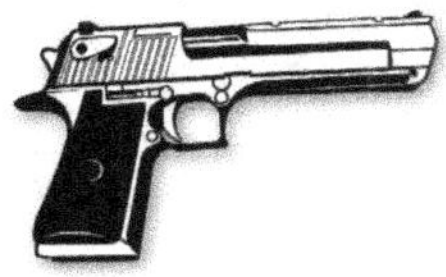

Chapter Eleven

Boulder Dam Lodge

Quint stopped pacing long enough to make a decision. "Okay, let's get back to business. You guys get back out on the street and find Yancy and Bernice. Jesse and I will check out the Hacienda lead before it gets stale. If you stumble onto something, communication is the word here. If they've found trouble, report and wait for backup. But if you think there isn't time, take appropriate action. Let's do it!"

Jesse remarked, "Those two pukes who kidnapped me came over the dam, so they must have gone by the hotel. As I remember the Hacienda was the last hotel on the Strip years ago."

"You're right, Jesse. Someone must have bought the rights to the name, or the old owners acquired this property and used the old name. Pull up to the hotel entrance at the far end towards the dam. That's where the lobby and registration desk are located."

Jesse drove the sedan under the entrance canopy, looking for the valet or doorman, but there was neither. "Must be slow, or someone is missing out on a good location to promote a valet job."

Quint said, "I'll check with the front desk people and see if they recognize our friends' pictures. You can hang out here and watch everyone who goes in and out. Hopefully, if they are here, we won't bump into them just yet."

Jesse pulled the car directly across from the front and shut the engine off, as people were walking in the designated pedestrian walkway, and he didn't want to share the car's exhaust.

Quint entered the hotel looking for the front desk. He didn't have to look far; it was just inside the sliding glass doors. There was no line at check-in. He approached a scholarly looking desk clerk. "Hello, young man, where can I find the manager on duty?"

"Welcome to the Hacienda, sir. I'm the manager on duty. How may I help you?"

Quint said, "I'm with a private investigation company, and I'd like show you a couple of pictures of two missing persons. They are thought to be in the Vegas valley somewhere, and you're the last resort hotel to be checked. Hopefully they are here or you have at least seen them."

"Sir, in order to give out any information on our guests, I'll need to see some identification. 'What happens in Las Vegas, stays in Las Vegas.' You know what I mean?"

"I work for a private, worldwide company specializing in missing persons. These guys may not be guests, so you won't be breaking any rules if you have seen them and tell me."

"I need to cover my ass here, sir, to be frank."

Quint knew this guy was not an amateur, so he pulled out his phony ID with a hundred dollar bill on the underside.

The manager smiled when he saw the ID and its companion, and said, "That ID looks official enough; show me the pictures."

Quint took the pictures out of the manila envelope and handed them to the manager. He looked them over without any expression on his face and handed them back to Quint. "I may have seen these guys. They do look familiar. Can't recall exactly when it was."

Quint put another hundred under the pictures and handed them back to the guy. "Maybe you should take another look."

He took the pictures, and the C-note disappeared into his jacket pocket. With a slight grin, he said, "My memory is getting better."

Quint replied, "It better blossom soon, pal, because the green has peaked. Make up your mind."

The manager could see the money trail had ended and the guy was getting a little testy, so he shot back, "Okay, you don't have to get huffy. They are staying here on the ninth and eleventh floors. The two are rude, arrogant, antagonistic, and cheap. I can give you the exact room numbers if you like."

"I like."

He walked over to the computer and quietly said, "Rooms 950 and 1150."

Quint gave the manager another hundred and said, "Keep this to yourself. It's very important these guys don't know we know they are here. There will be more folding money if things go well, as we might need your assistance again."

The manager said, "You'll have my undivided attention."

"No need to tell anyone else of our inquiries. Let's keep this close to the vest. There will be myself and a few others in and out. Just act normal, and we'll get along fine."

"Yes sir. Anything I can do for you will be my pleasure."

Quint was thinking, *What a great city! Everyone has great memories and deep pockets. Cash is king.*

"Do you know if they are in the hotel right now? Which side of the building are the rooms on?"

"No, I just came on duty, and the rooms are on the side towards the helipad."

"Okay, thanks."

Quint couldn't believe their good fortune in finding the duo so easily. Heading out the door, he waved at Jesse to fire up the limo.

Jumping in, he said, "Pull over to the side of the building towards the helipad. We have struck the mother lode. Our two wayward pukes are staying in the hotel. Their rooms face towards the helicopter pad up there on the hill."

"Yeah, I see it. Twenty-nine bucks for a five-minute ride over the dam and lake; sounds reasonable enough."

Quint said, "It's about time we got lucky on something. We've been on Murphy's shit list for far too long.

"Pull into one of those parking spaces near the road to Hoover Dam. We can see the front entrance and the windows in the high-rise. I'm familiar with the hotel; there is no back entrance, but the west end has access to the casino. We'll do a recon when we get some help and keep an eye on both entrances. Allowing our quarry to slip away again will not happen. It would be better to kill them."

The hotel was a Mecca of sorts for boaters from Arizona and California, with the parking lot full of expensive boats on three-axle trailers. I hope the Hacienda is not on the terrorists' list for destruction.

"I'll give the team a call with the good news, and hopefully, they'll tell us Yancy and Bernice have returned," said Quint.

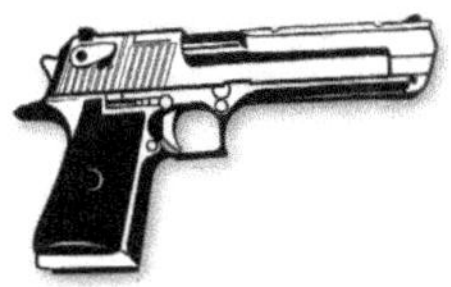

Chapter Twelve

Allies

As Yancy was about to yell out to get the attention of the hookah proprietor, he and one of the waiters walked through the swinging doors to the temporary hoosegow.

Bernice shouted at them, "Release us immediately! You don't know who you're dealing with!" Her loud, angry voice startled them, and they both jumped back, confirming what she and Yancy thought: they were amateurs caught up in a situation way over their heads.

The waiter turned to run out of the kitchen, but the owner grabbed him and spoke sternly in their native tongue. *"She is not dead. We have to kill them. We must behead the infidels for killing our brothers!"*

The waiter was petrified; he had turned white at the suggestion of more killing. *"We cannot kill them. What will we do with the bodies? Someone will come looking for them. They are not average people. The woman is well-trained. You saw how easily she disposed of our skilled comrades!"*

They just looked at each other in a quandary about what to do next.

Bernice whispered, "What did they say?"

Yancy whispered back, "They are confused about what to do. Now might be a good time to suggest something to get them off the hook and give us our freedom."

In a calmer voice, Bernice said, "Hey, let's talk about the present situation. We are professionals, as you can see by the deaths of your friends. They have led you down a path you may not have wanted to go.

"We can offer you a way out of this mess, and you can get back to your normal lives. The brotherhood will not find out what took place here."

The two amateurs looked at each other. The waiter said, "How will you guarantee your proposal?"

The owner shouted at the waiter, and they began to argue, highly agitated, waving, and pointing around the room. Then just as quickly as they started, they stopped.

"What the hell did they say, Yancy?" whispered Bernice.

"The waiter said, 'We are not soldiers, we were led into this mess with false bravado. Let's hear their offer. Are you prepared to lose all you have worked for? Your family and mine hang in the balance between our new home here and finding paradise before we are ready.' "

Bernice shouted at the two, "We will dispose of the bodies, not turn you in to the local authorities, and keep what has happened here between the four of us and our team. And furthermore, you tell us what those two stiffs were planning, and how many more are involved. Before you decide your future, remember our friends are presently looking for us. They will find us one way or another, and I'm sure you want to be on the right side when that happens. You'll never see paradise in the manner you may desire if they find us harmed in any way. Your people will not find out what happened here today. Untie us!"

The two men turned and walked back through the swinging doors without saying a word. Muffled sounds came through the doors, not clear enough for Yancy to translate.

After a few minutes, the doors swung open. "We want to hear the details of your proposal," said the waiter. The owner's face didn't show his support for the decision, but he nodded in agreement.

Yancy remarked, "Old Surly Face will need to be watched. He looks like someone who just swallowed a cup of turpentine."

The waiter bent down and cut the bonds, allowing them to stand. Bernice wobbled a bit. Yancy held her up until the cobwebs disappeared.

Yancy said, "Okay, give us our cellphones, so we can get this mess cleaned up. Is our vehicle still parked outside?"

"Yes," answered the waiter.

"Oh, that's great. I hope I can get our people on the phone before they come in here shooting. If they do, you and your boss will be killed in the blink of an eye, which will draw unwanted attention to this place."

Jake and Jett were cruising the hookah bars when Jett shouted, "There's their car!"

Jake made a quick turn into the parking lot. They parked a few cars away and waited a few minutes to see if anyone approached the vehicle. With no activity around the vehicle or the bar, they decided to inspect the car and look for signs of a struggle.

Jett said, "Well, they didn't have a problem here with the car. Let's call Sue and Keno for backup. When they get here, we'll go in the front and back. They must have found trouble, or we would have heard from them by now."

Jake went around to the rear to cover the bar's six, while Jett watched the front. Not more than fifteen minutes later Sue and Keno pulled into the lot, parking next to Bernice's car.

Jett walked over and explained the situation. "We think Bernice and Yancy are in the bar. Sue, Jake's around back; you join him. Keno and I will go in the front door and see what's up. If you hear a ruckus or gunfire, come in and give us a hand."

When Yancy began to punch the cell, the owner panicked and began shooting at him and Bernice. They hit the deck with the bullets bouncing off the kitchen equipment in all directions.

Sue and Keno were approaching the kitchen door when the shots rang out. They burst through the door in time to see the waiter hit the deck with his hands over his ears, yelling something lost in the confusion.

Sue put two bullets in the owner's forehead as Jett and Jake entered through the swinging doors from the front.

The owner fell to the floor on his way to wherever he thought paradise was, while Bernice, still a little woozy, managed to get to her feet with a flesh wound to her thigh from one of the ricocheting bullets. "Damn, there I go again. A walking target for every crazy son of a bitch with a weapon. Shit! Shot with my own gun."

Jett looked around and remarked, "Looks like you guys had a bit of a problem. Who are the stiffs?"

Yancy answered, "The two by the sink are hard-core terrorists, and the one Sue shot was throwing in with the dead guys. He used to own the bar. The guy with the apron is a waiter and didn't want any part of the kidnapping, killing, or joining in with the bad guys. He might be able to tell us something about what they were planning to do here."

Jett picked up the waiter and asked him, "The former owner who is now on his way to wherever— was he married?"

"Yes."

"Call his wife and tell her that some terrorists have killed her husband, and if she says a word to anyone, she and her children will be executed."

The waiter did as he was told.

When the waiter finished talking with the widow, Jett asked, "Do you know what these three were planning? I suggest you come clean with us, or you'll find yourself buried in a ditch."

In a voice that sounded more like a young teenager, the waiter spoke rapidly and almost unintelligibly. "They were to meet a couple of other people here, the masterminds behind their mission. There are also more coming. I believe the others are coming through Laughlin and a place called Sandy Valley. I don't know the details, but the two they were to meet are here now. Where the meeting was to take place I don't know."

"Can you run this hookah bar?"

"Yes."

"You take over the business and run it like nothing happened. We'll clean the mess up. You will be watched 24/7. One false move, and you will disappear."

"I understand. I don't want any trouble with you or the brotherhood terrorists."

"Jake, get Quint on the cell and explain the situation here."

Just as Jake was typing in Quint's number, his cell barked.

"Jake, Quint here. We have good news, but before I share that, did you find our lost souls?"

"Yes, we did." Jake went on to explain what had taken place. "What do you suggest?"

"We'll have to keep close tabs on the bar. I'll call the Cabal for a clean-up crew. Is there a walk-in cooler there? If there is, put the stiffs in there for safekeeping until the crew arrives. How bad is Bernice?"

"She's okay, just a flesh wound, and her ego has been bruised. What's the good news from your end?"

Quint relayed the scene at the Hacienda.

"Tell the others to go back to the safe house as soon as you guys get things squared away there. You come out to the hotel. We need someone to help keep tabs on the entrances. As you said, there are more people coming and they will be wondering, along with our friends at the hotel, what happened to two of their own. It also sounds like we need to provide protection to the waiter—he's stuck his neck in the wringer giving us a hand. Have Yancy stay outside the bar and watch for any bad guys who may show up. Jesse and I will be at either end of the hotel. Can Bernice take care of her wounds?"

Jake smiled and responded, "Yeah, she can handle it, but it's gonna take a big band-aid for that bruised ego."

When Jake arrived at the Hacienda, Quint went on to apprise him of how things stood.

"Okay this is what we have so far. The two who took a powder on us have rooms on the ninth and eleventh floors. The windows face the helipad on the hill there."

Jake asked, "Are they in the hotel right now?"

"Without valet parking, we don't have a source for their comings and goings. The hotel manager didn't notice if they were in or not. He called the rooms, but didn't get an answer. That doesn't mean much, since they probably won't be using the house phones."

As they stood in the parking lot, Jake looked around and suggested, "How about we walk up to the helicopter pad and see what the location looks like from on high? The high ground is generally an advantageous position."

Quint walked over to his car to retrieve his binoculars, and they hoofed it over to the helicopter ticket sales building to inquire about taking a hike up to the chopper landing pad.

Jake gave the saleslady a nice crispy hundred-dollar bill. "My friend and I would like to look over the lake from your helicopter landing area. It has a much better view than from down below at the hotel."

She was happy to oblige the two young men as she stuffed the new bill into her bra, without the slightest appearance of embarrassment.

It was a steep climb up to the pad, but worth the hike because of the unobstructed view of the hotel room windows with the binoculars.

As Quint was scanning the rooms on the ninth floor, he found Najib standing at the far end window gabbing away on a cellphone.

Quint moved up two floors and checked out the other room on the eleventh floor. The curtains were open, and there was someone asleep in bed. *Bingo!* Quint said, "That must be Mahathir. We have two birds in the cage. They don't seem too concerned about leaving the curtains open. I guess they figure being up so high, no one can see in."

Jake said, "We need to bug the rooms and intercept their cell conversations—or just kill them and be done with it!"

"Nice thought, we could easily take them out from here, no problem," said Quint, "but we need to find out who the others are and where they are, before they do something dastardly."

"Maybe we kill these two and with the other two at the hookah bar dead, it will cramp their style, and the rest of them will head home," replied Jake.

"More likely they would regroup. When you intend to kill yourself and take as many others with you as you can, there's not much that will keep you from doing just that. They win, we lose. We need to throw a big net and kill them all."

"Okay, Quint. It was just a thought—end this as soon as possible without loss of life on our part. What a pleasure it would be to squeeze the trigger and watch the rounds take them down."

"Jake, we have to give them enough rope to hang themselves. Give their cohorts around the world something to remember on the anniversary of their failed attempt and quick demise. A message that we are out here and will fuck them up. I'll give Jesse a call and tell him we have our prey under surveillance."

Quint punched Jesse's number. "Jesse, take the car and head back to the house. Jake is here. We'll stay and keep an eye on the scumbags.

"We'll need to bring out some equipment to bug the rooms and monitor their cell phones. Tell the gang what's up."

"Ten-four, see you guys later."

"Okay, okay! Jesus you guys! I can handle it!" Bernice was almost yelling as everyone tried to play doctor with her wounds. "I've been shot before. It just seems to be getting a little too regular lately."

About the time everything settled down in the house, Jesse popped in. "Quint and Jake have our quarry under a watchful eye." He went on to explain what was needed at the hotel.

Bernice shot back, "Can they see into the rooms?"

"I don't know, I was at the other end of the building the whole time."

Bernice keyed in Quint's number.

"Quint here."

"Quint." Before she could say anything, Quint interrupted, "Well, I hear you acquired another wound."

"Can the chatter, Quint. I have some serious questions."

"Okay, don't be so touchy."

"Quint!"

"Yes, what's on your mind, Bernice?"

"Can you see into the rooms?"

"Yes. As a matter of fact, they are on the upper floors, and they left the curtains open. Our friends feel very safe that high up, I guess."

"With binoculars, can you see their faces up close? Like, can you see their lips moving?"

"Sure. What the hell are you getting at?"

"Yancy reads lips and understands their language. He could come out there and maybe while we are setting up the other stuff, he can give us a heads-up on what they're planning."

"Damn, that could be some asset, not only out here, but there will be many occasions where that would come in handy. Have Yancy come to the hotel. We are on the side facing the helipad. Tell him I'll meet him at the helicopter tour ticket office."

"Okay."

When Yancy arrived at the helicopter office, Quint said, "Let's walk up to the helipad. How is the guy who helped us out at the hookah bar?"

"I don't think he will survive throwing his lot in with us. I suspect his kind will figure he ratted them out and kill him. There may not be a way to keep him from finding paradise, unless one of us is with him 24/7. You're the experts, you tell me."

Quint responded, "You may be right, Yancy. We can't babysit this guy around the clock. I'll ask Sue to go there and talk him into taking a powder. The Cabal can find a safe place for him until we eliminate the threat. Who took your place at the bar?"

"Sue."

Quint typed in Sue's number.

"Sue here."

"Sue, talk to the hookah guy and see if he's willing to leave town under the care of the Cabal until we get things squared away here. If he's okay with that, give our people a call and arrange for him and his family to disappear."

"The process is already in play. Our thoughts seem to run along the same lines—in a variety of different and exciting ways, but most of that has to be put on hold."

"Okay, thanks. See you back at the house."

Quint closed the cell as they reached the helipad. Yancy asked, "Can they really hide this guy?"

"Sure."

Quint handed Yancy his binoculars and said, "Check the rooms out."

Yancy took a quick look at the rooms in the tower. "I can see well enough to read lips. As a matter of fact, I'm looking at a man and his wife screaming at each other about his losing money they didn't have."

Quint said, "Go to the room on the far end of the ninth floor, and see if Najib is home."

Yancy scanned the ninth floor left to right, seeing some interesting scenes, but not lingering.

"He's home and standing in the center of the window, yakking on the phone. The lips say our subject is ordering a pizza. I thought these guys had a strict Middle East-style diet. Maybe they are only rigid when it suits them. They'll be at a topless bar next. Could be if they get into our culture a bit more, they might not want to destroy their new discovery."

Quint replied, "I think you're right, they do things when it's convenient. However, I don't look for them to declare their independence anytime soon. Their wish for us to die is at the top of their agenda and not likely to change. Move up two floors just above Najib and you'll find Mahathir's room. See what's up with him."

Moving up two floors, Yancy reported, "The room is lighted, but no activity. Maybe he's in the bathroom."

"You hang out here and keep an eye on them. I'm heading back to the safe house. I'll send Jesse back to help you in case they decide to leave and go in different directions. Give me a call if anything changes."

"Ten-four."

Just as Quint was heading down the steep path, Yancy yelled, "Hold on, Najib is talking to someone about an arrival."

Quint sprinted back up the hill, dodging a helicopter taking off for its short tour of the dam and Lake Mead, to join Yancy as he translated the conversation.

"He's saying that two new guys will be coming in through Bullhead City's small airport. Shit! He just turned around. Son of a bitch! It would be nice if he were tied up facing the window. You know, after we get what we can from him, we should go up there and throw his ass out the window."

Quint asked, "He didn't give any times, nothing more?"

"No, but he's turned back around. His attitude has changed though—like he's a little pissed off at whoever he's talking to. He just mentioned Bullhead City again, yelling something about not using any Nevada or California charter services. He's just listening now, nodding his head every couple of breaths.

"Okay, he's just given us the flight information: There will be a four-seater coming in tomorrow night with two more bad guys aboard. The flight will arrive around midnight from Tucson. These cockroaches always do their nasty shit at night. That makes four, six if you include the two stiffs at the hookah bar."

Yancy moved his binoculars up to check on Mahathir, but he was still not visible. "I think they need more people. The hard part for us is to decide when to take them down. The airport in Bullhead City is not very busy, so we won't have any trouble seeing who is who."

Quint said, "I'm going to head back now. Keep me posted. Jesse should be here shortly."

Yancy kept the binoculars trained on Najib's head, but he kept pacing back and forth, turning first one way and then the other.

"Okay, I'll keep in contact with these slimeballs. You know they'll want to be at the airport when their friends arrive. Maybe we should just do them all there and be done with it."

"Yancy, I keep telling you guys we need to know how many there are and where they plan to strike. We can't kill half the team. These people will die gladly for some imagined glory they think will come to them. So when the time is right, we'll help them find their god and all his rewards."

"Okay, okay, you're the expert."

"We'll give them enough rope to hang themselves," repeated Quint.

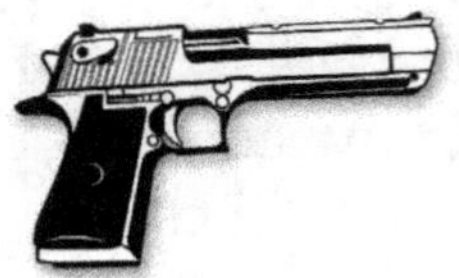

Chapter Thirteen

Sandy Valley

When Quint returned to the house, everyone was present except for Yancy, Jesse, and Sue. He yelled for everyone to gather around. "We have our quarry under surveillance at the Boulder Dam Lodge out by the dam. Yancy is reading lips for now, and so far we have two more guys flying into Bullhead City tomorrow night. We'll follow Najib and Mahathir to the airport and see who arrives. I'm sure this isn't the last to fill their ranks."

Jake spoke up, "Jett and I have the equipment ready to install in their rooms as soon as they leave. We'll be able to monitor their cells, house phones, and the conversations in both rooms. We might even be able to put some small devices in their clothing to track them in case they get lucky and we lose them in a crowd."

While they were deciding what to do next, Quint's cell interrupted him. "Quint here."

Yancy was on the other end. "Our targets have some type of explosives arriving in Sandy Valley tonight. Guess they like the valley, even though I gave them some unpleasant memories there. They're talking a midnight drop-off. There are no landing lights out there. I don't know how they purpose to get down in the dark!"

Quint asked, "Since you're the flying expert, what are their options?"

"There are no options. If you can't see the runway, you will most likely crash land your plane. Pilot error! There is one way to find out. We can be there to see how they manage."

Quint turned to the others after relaying Yancy's report and asked, "Well? Any ideas on this one?"

No one raised their hand. Quint said into the phone, "Guess we'll have to wait and see. Yancy, when they leave the hotel give us a shout and Keno and I will head out to the valley. We want to be there before they arrive. Jake and Jett, you go take care of business in the hotel rooms."

Sue threw her hands in the air. "The Cabal will protect you! If you stay here, your brotherhood will have no qualms about killing you and your family. It's not nice to drop a dime on your loving brothers. They have only one thing on their mind, to kill and destroy the West, whether you are in the picture or not. Two are dead, with more to follow. It's not complicated, my friend. You and your wife have an opportunity to mature to a ripe old age and watch your children and grandchildren grow up."

"Okay, if we decide to take you up on the offer, what happens to the business?"

"Now you're talking! The Cabal will buy it from the owner's wife and close the doors. When things settle down, and the bad guys are all on their way to paradise, they'll sell it back to her at a discounted price. Piece of cake."

The waiter was not a happy camper. He wished the infidels and the brotherhood had never come into the bar. Now his whole life was going to be turned upside down, and he could see an early death for himself. His only hope was their offer. Pondering his options, he threw his hands into the air and said, "Okay, let's do it."

Sue let out a sigh of relief. "You have made a wise decision for you and your family. Call your wife and tell her to expect a car to pick up the family. She'll be allowed only the clothes on her back, identification, and small mementos she can carry."

"Yeah, Yancy?"

"They're on the move, Quint."

"Okay. Is Jesse there?"

"Yes."

"Listen. Be careful as you tail them."

"Ten-four."

"Have you thought about how they intend to land in the dark?"

"There is no way to come down safely in the dark."

"Did you see their accomplice, Mohammed?"

"No, just the two. They're in their car now; actually, it's a half-ton Chevy pickup heading out your way."

"Okay, we're leaving now. We'll be there when they arrive."

Yancy looked over at Jesse. "The team is heading for Sandy Valley. Guess it's time for the rubber to hit the road. Wish we could just do these guys and call it a win."

Luckily for Jesse and Yancy, there were two cars between them and Najib, keeping Najib oblivious to their tail. Hopefully the cars separating them wouldn't split off and continue on to Goodsprings instead of Sandy Valley.

Quint said to the assembled team, "We fucked up losing track of Mohammed. That was inexcusable. He's a loose cannon, something we need to mend. Bernice, you stay here and hold down the fort. Jake, Jett, head over to the hotel and plant your stuff. Keno, bring the limo around, we need to get out to Sandy Valley."

Keno was happy to be on the road, instead of hanging at the safe house. Taking the old LA highway, he made good time to Jean and after passing under the I-15 overpass, he headed up the road toward Goodsprings and over the mountain to Sandy Valley.

It was nearly midnight when Keno drove the limo onto the valley floor. He doused the lights and parked behind the large maintenance hangar to wait for Najib

158

to show up. As they waited, a figure could be seen walking along the tarmac, dropping flares.

Quint spoke up. "I guess we know where Mohammed is! He must be the guiding light for our friends with the explosive-laden airship. He's dropping flares along the runway."

Quint called Yancy. "When you guys get to Kingston Road, hang back until you hear from us."

As Mohammed struck the last flare, the drone of a motor could be heard coming in from the west.

"You hear that, Keno? Sounds like our bird is about to face the challenge of touching down in the middle of nowhere, in the dark, with six highway flares for lights."

"Yeah, I hear him. Do you think we should slide down into the grease pit on the side of the building? If he fucks up the landing it might be a good place if the plane is laden with some type of HE."

As they were about to run to the side of the maintenance building, the plane throttled back, the wheels touched down, bounced up, the engine revved up, and then the plane settled down.

The pilot idled to the far end of the runway, performed a one-eighty, and stopped. Mohammed ran up and pulled the door open, helping the pilot down.

Quint got on the cell and called Yancy and Jesse. "You guys come down near the airstrip and park close to one of the hangars just off the road. I'll let you know if you need to take action or just follow."

"Okay, we're on the way. Najib is just ahead of us," replied Jesse.

Keno poked Quint in the back. "Look at those dumbasses down there yelling and arm waving at each other. What the hell do you think they're so upset about? Shit, I thought any landing short of death was a good one."

"Hell! Who knows about those wingnuts."

The headlights of a vehicle could be seen coming down Kingston Road. Quint figured it was Najib and his halfwit partner. "Those lights must be Najib; he's just ahead of Jesse."

When the lights turned onto the runway, Quint said, "It must be him. Our wingnuts have stopped yelling and waving their arms at each other."

As they watched Najib's truck find its way down the tarmac, the pilot climbed back into the plane and began to hand Mohammed small bricks, which he stacked near the wheels.

Najib pulled up to the plane and yelled something at the two, who then began to put the small bricks back into the plane. When the loading was completed, Najib started finger pointing, scolding the pilot, who in turn pointed at Mohammed. As the circus continued, the pilot jumped back into the plane, fired up the engine, and with the small truck leading the way, the truck-plane convoy headed back up the tarmac. As the convoy approached the maintenance hangar they turned right towards the first of a row of hangars on a long runway-street combo;

160

it was huge, capable of holding at least three planes, with a large second-floor deck extending from the middle all the way around to the rear, where the living quarters were located. As they neared the private hangar, the automatic doors opened up, allowing the truck and plane to enter. The small convoy disappeared behind the enormous doors, leaving the area in complete darkness when they closed.

"Jesus," said Keno. "They must have bought or rented the hangar. We've been watching them damn near 24/7. When did they have time to do that?"

Quint replied, "It must have been Mohammed. I'm happy they have it. We know where the hell they are, and it's a sure bet Najib will be using this place to store whatever evil is up his sleeve."

Quint got on the cell. "Jesse, you and Yancy come to the maintenance hangar. We'll be waiting for you there. Our quarry has found a new home."

When Yancy and Jesse arrived at the maintenance hangar, Quint called for a meeting of the minds. "Our friends have found a new home across the tarmac in that huge hangar. We need to recon the place for all possible ways in and out. Yancy, there's a small window in the door used for foot traffic. Head over there and with all the stealth you can muster, peer in and see if you can read some lips and find out what they're up to.

"The rest of us will fan out and search the area. Take a half hour or so, and then we'll all meet back here. Let's go."

"I told you to bring the Yperite gas, not the Semtex! We want to go after the huge cooling systems in a couple of hotels to terrorize the city before we bring down our targets and make the World Trade Center pale in comparison."

Yancy was doing his best to read the conversations. As usual, no one stood still facing him, but he read enough to know they had some serious shit on their agenda.

Najib continued, "We'll offload the Semtex and store it here. Take the fucking plane back to New Mexico and bring back the Yperite gas. Do not make another mistake, or your punishment will be a visit with the virgins, and your family will make the trip with you."

The pilot turned and climbed into his plane. Mohammed flipped the switch to open the hangar doors and allow the small four-seater to exit onto the tarmac.

Yancy had to slip away and watch from a position behind a clump of sagebrush. He was joined by Keno, Quint, and Jesse, who, upon seeing the hangar doors begin to open, had also headed for cover.

When they were all gathered behind the sagebrush, Yancy explained the situation the best he could, and everyone got the idea. Keno remarked, "I guess we know why they were yelling and arm waving earlier. What the hell is Yperite?"

Quint spoke up. "Yperite is more commonly known as mustard gas or blister gas. Its use was perfected during WWI. The gas will put the fear of God into anyone who gets stung by it. They must be depending on ventilation systems to spread it quickly and with as many casualties as possible before they get the serious stuff on target. If their goal is to terrorize before the Semtex starts, Yperite is a good choice. They create a diversion with the mustard gas, and then when everyone has gathered to help the victims, they pull the trigger on the Semtex."

As the plane throttled up and sped down the runway, lifting off to disappear into the night, Najib could be heard yelling at his hapless cohort and Mohammed.

Yancy translated for the team, still hidden behind the sagebrush. "He's really pissed about the idiot pilot, who has now put them behind schedule by two days. He told Mohammed to get back to town and meet with the others and tell them what happened. They're going to keep the hangar for their HQ and storage facility. He and Mahathir are going back to the Hacienda. Hopefully, the room bugs will work. It's hard to read lips when the speaker is moving around."

As the hangar doors began to close, Najib's vehicle sped out ahead of Mohammed's car toward Kingston Road and town.

Quint said, "Yancy, you and Keno follow Mohammed to see where their fellow terrorists are holed up. Jesse and I will stay glued to Najib."

Chapter Fourteen

The Tail

"Hey, they're pulling into the Mandalay Bay," yelled Yancy. "We have to stay close or we'll lose him in the crowd. Looks like he's using valet parking. That's a good thing. Easy to keep track of him, and he'll never know we're here. The Shadow knows, but he's not here to spill the beans."

Keno pulled closer to Mohammed's car. The morning sun glinted in his eyes. "What the hell is the shadow knows?"

"It's a radio program from the thirties. The Shadow knew everything about everybody and haunted the people he thought needed a wake-up call. Good program but now in the dustbin of history."

Waiting in line, Keno noted, "Mohammed must have given the valet guy a nice toke; he's putting his car up front."

As they watched, Mohammed walked up to the house phone and made a short call, then returned to the valet for his keys and another tip.

"Damn, we won't know who, what, or where. Shit!" Yancy whispered.

"Why are you whispering?" said Keno. "They can't hear us."

"I'm speaking quietly because I would like to throttle that little puke. We need to know how many are here and what their room numbers are. The phone call doesn't help us one bit. It would be nice to bitch slap that scumbag just before we send him to the virgins."

Mohammed turned south out of the driveway, but made a U-turn at the end of the divider. Keno followed, and the two cars headed north up the Strip.

Yancy said, "Good for us there's a lot of traffic on the Strip. Mohammed will never know we're behind him."

"Look at that, will you? He's pulling into the Flamingo. Damn, I hope he goes inside and up to a room," said Keno.

The same routine took place as they waited in the limo parking area. He paid the valet, made a call on the house phone and left, heading north.

Yancy said, "Damn, now he's heading into the Treasure Island. How many people are we dealing with? If he doesn't do anything but call, we'll never know. Shit!"

Once again it was park, toke the valet, use the house phone, and then head back north up the Strip.

Keno said, "Well, here we go again. I suppose the Sahara is as good as any for his people to hang out. Same routine here. I wonder where he's staying?"

"We should find out soon. There he goes again, heading downtown."

They followed Mohammed down the Strip toward Fremont Street, where he turned right. The traffic was not nearly as heavy on Fremont so they had to stay back a little further. As they approached Fifteenth Street there was a traffic jam, with cops and ambulances all over the place in the hooker and drug infested end of Fremont. During the confusion, Mohammed slipped away, leaving his car parked in the line of vehicles waiting for the okay to proceed.

"He's jumped ship," said Yancy. "We'll never catch that shitbird in this mess. Fuck! I don't think he's as dumb or as arrogant as his cohorts."

Keno turned the car around and headed back to the safe house to share their tale of woe.

Najib headed his small truck back up Kingston Road towards Columbia Pass and Vegas. Quint and Jesse hoped he would lead them to some more bad guys, so they would have some idea how big of a net it would take to shut them down. Putting them out of business without causing a panic in the city would become a problem if the numbers were big.

Quint noted, "He's not making any attempt to look for a tail. These guys are so cocksure, they think they're invisible."

Najib slipped under I-15, passed the casino on the right and then took a left at the stop sign on the old LA highway at the extreme south end of Las Vegas Boulevard. The old-timers would call it Fifth Street.

Quint's cell buzzed for attention. "Quint here."

Keno was on the other end with the report on Mohammed. "Our guy stopped at numerous hotels going north on the Strip. He pulled into valet at each hotel, used valet, and made one phone call per hotel. We don't have a clue what he said or who he talked to. We lost him on Fremont Street in a traffic jam. He may have spotted us. The asshole jumped out of his car and hoofed it. We're headed back to the safe house."

"That's not good news," responded Quint. "See you at the house."

Jesse said, "What the hell was that all about? You don't look happy, Quint."

Quint explained, and Jesse remarked, "We know which hotels they're in."

"We won't know them from sour apples. We have to follow them from Sandy Valley when they distribute the gas and C-4."

"He's turned off toward Boulder City and the Hacienda," said Jesse. "The guys should have the rooms bugged by now, so maybe we can find out more details. I'll call Jake and let them know that Najib is on the way."

Quint didn't follow Najib, but headed for the safe house to meet up with the gang and figure their next move.

"Who was that, Jake?" asked Jett.

"That was Jesse. Najib is heading for the hotel, and he figures to be about fifteen minutes out. We have just enough time to finish up. They won't be able to pass air without us knowing."

"Okay, that's it Jake. Let's head back over to the helipad to wait for them to show and see how the readings go," said Jett as he headed for the door.

Just as they exited into the hallway, the elevator door at the opposite end of the hall opened and Najib stepped out. Jake and Jett turned their backs and tried to appear to be looking out the window at the end of the hall. Najib, always on the paranoid side, asked, "Can I be of some service to you gentlemen?"

Jett responded, "No thank you, sir. We're just checking our boats in the parking lot. The lighting on this end is way better than the other. We made a good choice parking the boats down there."

Najib didn't look convinced with their story, but keyed his room and entered.

They headed down the hall, not saying anything until the elevator doors closed.

Jake spoke first. "Well, do you think we were made?"

"I don't think he made us, but he's been put on alert," responded Jett. "We need to get Yancy out here. In the meantime we'll tape all the conversations. He's probably on the phone already. Shit!"

They made their way up to the helipad, and with binoculars and recorders in hand began the stakeout.

Jake got on his cell. "Quint, we need Yancy at the hotel. We finished bugging the rooms and Najib is already on the phone. He showed up a lot quicker than you thought, and we met in the hallway." He went on to explain the meeting. "Can you get Yancy out here ASAP?"

"Yes, I'm sending him as we speak. How is the equipment working?"

"The equipment is doing fine. He's on the phone right now with someone who has agitated the hell out of him. We don't know what he's saying, but he sounds like someone about to blow a gasket."

"Okay, hang in there, Yancy is on the way. If anything earth shattering comes up, get right back to me."

"Ten-four."

Quint said, "Okay, gang, let's sit down and share what we have to date. The Hacienda is covered inside and out, so we can be sure what Najib is up to.

"Bernice, Sue, what's up with you guys? Bernice, are you all healed up and ready for more action?"

Sue spoke first. "Yes, let's get moving on something."

Bernice chimed in, "It's time to get this ball rolling. What's our next move?"

Quint was still not sure the girls were in good enough shape to handle any close combat situations.

"I want you two to head out to Sandy Valley and keep an eye on the hangar Najib is using for his other headquarters. There could be a flight coming in there at any time."

He went on to explain in detail their encounter in the valley and how important it was to keep a close eye on the property.

Sue shot back, "You think giving us that babysitting job will keep us from anything physical? We are not ready to be put out to pasture!"

"Bernice could use a little more time to heal, and besides, until we get more information from our taps on Najib, we're more or less spinning our wheels. But like I said, you might have some visitors out there before we know anything more here. So be good scouts. Find your way out there and keep in touch."

Bernice and Sue were not pleased with the turn of events, but when they were alone heading for Sandy Valley, Bernice said, "You know, I do need some time to heal, and besides, we might get some action no one is expecting."

Sue remarked, "Quint doesn't think you are up to speed yet, and I can understand that, but I don't like the idea of not being at ground zero."

"Yancy, did I hear you right? Did he say six helicopters?"

"Yes, he did, Jett."

"Where the hell would they get six helos, and what the fuck for?"

"I don't know. The last sentence wasn't clear, and he's turned his back to me again. Shit!"

Yancy listened a moment and then spoke slowly. "He said six helicopters and then it got fuzzy, but it sounded like Sandy Valley were the last two words that tailed off at the end."

Jake spoke up. "Let's get Quint over here. Maybe by the time he arrives, we'll have something to add."

When Quint answered, Jake explained, "Quint, we have something that may need immediate attention. Could you come to the hotel?"

"On my way," said Quint as he turned to instruct Jesse, "You hang here and hold down the fort. I'm going out to the hotel."

Looking through the binoculars, Jett exclaimed, "There's Mahathir with Mohammad. That's a good thing. We know where everyone is now. We could just do these guys now and be done with it. What do you say, Quint?"

172

"You know we can't do anything, Jett, until we have all the players and their intentions in our sights. We need to send a worldwide message when we dust these fuckers. Let the assholes in terrorville know we have their number and will fuck them up every time they plan some evil deed."

"Ten-four," said Jett.

Chapter Fifteen

The Stakeout

"What's up now, Yancy?" asked Quint.

"Hold on; he's in the middle of an oration about their goals. He hasn't mentioned who had him so exercised earlier. Damn! Holy cow! Jesus!"

"Come on Yancy, quit fucking around and share all the wows with us."

"He's in the middle of it. I don't want to miss anything. Najib is facing me, and I'm getting his words in vivid color."

"That's the hangar we're looking for," said Bernice. "Damn, that's a huge building."

"Compared to the others, it could be sitting on more than one lot, with the exception of those buildings down there on the right," remarked Sue. "Looks like everything past that sand dune at the end of the tarmac is in the low-rent district that we came upon before turning onto Kingston. This is a typical rural desert valley, where the people living here are trying to get away from the crowds, rules, and regulations of the big city."

She continued, "Okay, here we are near the California-Nevada state line, and there are only three ways in and out of the valley. Over the pass where we came in, Kingston Road towards the south, or back north towards Pahrump, Nevada—and of course from above. The roads are gravel, except for the blacktop coming in and some of Kingston Road. Anyone coming or going will be noticed in the daytime by the dust clouds. At night we'll see any lights, so we have the advantage here to observe all directions plus the sky. Piece of cake, huh?"

"Quint suggested we observe our quarry from behind the maintenance hangar over there at the beginning of the runway," said Bernice.

"Okay, let's settle in and take on whatever or whoever comes our way," replied Sue.

"Well? What's up Yancy?" asked Quint again.

"You aren't going to believe this."

"Try me."

"Okay, here goes. The plan, or plans, go into orbit. First they are going to plant the mustard gas in four hotels on the Strip to get the ball rolling. When the chaos is at its peak, they are going to fly six highjacked helicopters into the top floors of the hotels they've chosen downtown. It will make it all the more difficult to get to the flames at the top of the buildings and create more confusion. When the discombobulation is at its peak, they're going to implode the New York-New York and bring it down like the World Trade Center. This is all supposed to happen on the anniversary of the New York twin towers event. The guy who had him so exercised on the phone was the one who fucked up the delivery of the gas and HE. There will be another delivery tonight. When the stockpile is completed, the bombers in the hotels will make a trip to Sandy Valley to pick up their share of the materials. There are supposed to be some explosives experts coming in from the east coast, by way of private aircraft. They will land at the Jean Airport."

"Damn! We may not have enough people to squash this attack, but if we notify the local authorities it will leak out and we'll have a full-scale fucking riot on our hands with panic in the streets. We have to figure a way to take care of business within our group," responded Quint.

Najib, speaking with authority, said, "Okay, that is the plan for now. You know as much as I do, and we'll carry out the will of God and be on our way to paradise as heroes. But our next move will be to change our residence. I met a couple of infidels in the hallway earlier, and they had the look of individuals hiding something. It may not mean anything, but we'll change to a more convenient location. The hotel in Jean on the road to Sandy Valley and Goodsprings will be more suited to our needs. We'll be closer to our storage facility and have more control of our people when they come out to pick up their share of the goods needed to destroy the city.

"Mahathir, you go down and check us out. We'll meet in the parking lot, load the vehicles, and use the old LA highway to Jean. Be most observant of your surroundings."

Yancy relayed the latest from Najib to Quint and the others.

"Shit, we just got the rooms bugged and everything is working fine. I hope Murphy is not going to horn in on our mission again," exclaimed Quint. "Jett, you and Jake head out to that hotel in Jean and hang out in the lobby. Bypass the front desk and follow them to their rooms. Yancy, let's take the tapes to the safe house, and review them to be sure we didn't miss anything. Okay, everybody. Chop-chop!"

"That's all of the tapes, and we haven't missed anything. Where do you suppose they're going to come up with six helicopters?" asked Yancy. "Choppers are not on sales lots anywhere near here."

Quint thought about the question for a few minutes and drew a blank. "I don't know."

Suddenly Yancy smiled "I think I know."

"Okay, let's hear it."

"There's a helicopter touring service at the end of the Strip. I believe they have more than six choppers there at any given time. That could be where they plan to find six birds. It would be easy enough to hire them for a Grand Canyon Tour and voila! Six human-guided missles."

"That all sounds good, but six Middle Eastern guys trying to hire six choppers would draw way too much attention."

"What if they didn't hire them, but walked into the office and took over? By the time Nellis Air Force base could be notified and scramble a couple of jets, the choppers would be in the air. It's only a two-minute flight to downtown. Those helicopters are sitting there warmed up for their daily flights. Piece of cake."

"You may have hit on something, Yancy. I wonder why they picked six, not two or three? One would create enough confusion downtown to draw all the emergency vehicles in the area and cause a huge traffic jam."

"Maybe they want to make sure at least one gets through if they're discovered."

"Could be. Well, for now, let's head out to Sandy Valley and see who shows up tonight. We can stop by and check with Jett at the hotel on the way. The bad guys should have checked in by now. We need to be in the valley before Najib and his cohorts get on the road. The sparse traffic on the Goodsprings Road makes it hard to tail anyone."

Jake's cell vibrated. "Jake here."

"Jake, did our bad guys check in?"

"Yeah, they're all in, top floor. We're in the lobby."

"Good. We'll be there in thirty minutes."

"Ten-four."

"That's your cell, Sue. You better put it on vibe or we might give ourselves away," whispered Bernice.

"Oh hell, I forgot. Sue here. Hello, Quint."

"Has anything shaken out there?"

"No."

"Okay. Jett, Jake, and I will be out to join you in an hour. Don't get into any trouble until you have some backup. Najib and his team are checked into the hotel at Jean. We'll leave Yancy at the hotel; hopefully, he can learn more about their plans."

"Okay, Quint. See you here."

Quint and Yancy arrived at the hotel in Jean to find Jake in the lobby. The casino was busy as usual, with the guests staying there instead of driving all the way into Vegas. The table games and slots paid the same, and the rooms were cheaper. The other benefit was the drive home, being ahead of the traffic coming from the Strip.

"Jake, how are the wannabe terrorists?"

Jake was sitting on the bench in the lobby checking out his keno ticket. "Our quarry are in their rooms."

"Where's Jett?"

"Jett's hanging out near the elevators. He'll give us a jingle if our people come down to the casino. I'm sure they'll be heading for Sandy Valley before long."

"Okay, listen. You, Jett, and I will head out to join Sue and Bernice. Yancy is going to stay at the hotel in case an opportunity presents itself to gain more information."

"Wait, Quint. They know Yancy. Wouldn't it be better if someone else stayed back?"

"That might be, but no one else can read lips. Yancy will have to be super careful."

"Okay, whatever you say, Quint."

"Yancy, go relieve Jett, and we'll head on out."

Yancy leaned up against a slot that backed up to the lobby area, and said, "Ten-four, and don't worry about me being made. I can blend into the casino crowd and read them from a good distance. I'll bring up the rear when the bad guys leave for the valley."

"Najib, the pilot called. The plane will be on time, and the cargo will be as requested. He will also bring along two extra people who are experts with the gas," said Mahathir.

"Okay. Good. Let's head down to the restaurant. We have enough time for a quick meal."

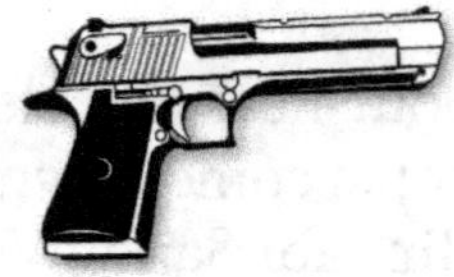

Chapter Sixteen

Yancy

"Najib, did you see that guy standing by the stairs? He looked very familiar."

"Yes, Mahathir, I did. That's the infidel pilot that we need to behead. He is not very good at spying. We can circle around through the dining room and come up behind him. He is obviously following us. I wonder how he found us?"

As they made their way to the dining room, Najib suggested, "I was thinking, maybe we don't kill him, but bribe him to keep us informed of what is going on with the people who are following us. He is a greedy capitalist without any moral character. The pig would sell his mother for a price. I can see it in his eyes. There is no loyalty to religion, country, or cause."

While Yancy was watching his prey, he thought of all the money these people would need to accomplish their goals, and it made that other little voice down deep begin to nudge him. He tried to suppress the urge being sent to his conscience, the urge to take advantage of the situation. With one last burst of no-conscience, he could settle down in a warm climate to live out his remaining years in the comfort that he had worked so hard for and richly deserved. He could approach the two wingnuts and make the deal of a lifetime. All this straight talking and leg work with the good guys had gotten him nothing but a headache. It was a lot easier and more profitable to walk on the dark side and not give a shit about anyone or anything but himself.

With riches so close you could spit on them, Yancy's greed overpowered his will to travel down the loyalty road. The straight-talking, patriotic nonsense that overwhelmed the group he'd fallen in with had become unbearable. It was time for a change.

He made sure Najib and his dimwitted partner would get a quick look at him as they headed for the restaurant, knowing they would recognize him and want to take revenge for their earlier meeting in the valley. It would open an opportunity to make a deal for some real money. The chump change he had gotten from them before wasn't worth spit.

Najib turned to Mahathir. "Where did the infidel go? He was just standing there in the hallway."

The words had not left Najib's lips before he felt the cold steel of a handgun against the back of his head.

"Hello, my old friend. How have you been?" asked Yancy, as he moved the pistol around to Najib's face, with the barrel settling between his eyes. He had them dead to rights.

"We need to talk. So turn around and walk back up to your room, unless of course you want to die without the fanfare of destroying a portion of the

184

infidels' homeland and without finding your way to the virgins in a glorious death, dying for nothing in the eyes of your fanatic bothers."

Najib thought about resisting, but decided he might be able to handle the pilot and behead him when he was no longer useful.

He remarked as he turned to retreat to his room, "We may not have much to talk about. You owe us a considerable amount of Yankee dollars. That will have to be considered first."

"Najib, you are on the losing end of a very powerful handgun, and I will set the rules for our little chat. Now get moving before I paint the walls of this hallway with your little demented brain."

The valley was near darkness as the sun slowly found its way behind the purplish mountains that protected the small population who wanted to be shed of the big city and the outside world.

"I see lights coming down Kingston Road," said Sue. "I hope it's some of the team, so we won't have to call for backup if things go awry."

Bernice remarked with sarcastic optimism, "What the hell could go wrong? Here we are in the middle of nowhere, looking at a landing strip only a fool would land on in the darkness, waiting for a plane that might have enough explosives or nerve gas to take out half of Las Vegas, and we don't even know who or how many are on it. Are they armed? Do they have heavy weapons? We don't know shit! For all we know the arriving plane could be a C-130 loaded to the gills with people who want to kill us."

"Bernice, a C-130 can't land here. The tarmac isn't long enough."

"I know, but it doesn't help. We don't have enough information."

"That must be Quint. The car turned onto the runway near the first hangar."

Bernice replied, "Hell, that could be anybody. Maybe someone with every intention of taking us out."

"Damn, Bernice, take a breath!"

Sue's cell vibed. "It's Quint, Jett, and Jake."

"I get the feeling we should go ahead and take Najib and his lame partner out and move on. There is an itch I can't scratch about this situation. Something is wrong with this picture. My instincts are usually right on. We need to snoop around, look behind the curtain," said Bernice.

"Okay, talk to Quint when they get here. Tell him about your instincts. He may have some new information."

Quint's sedan pulled up behind the maintenance building and parked beside Sue's car, both out of sight from the runway and hangar where Najib had his goods stored.

They all gathered around, but as Quint was about to speak his cell gave notice.

"Quint, Najib, along with his dimwitted partner and Mohammed, are on the way. They just left the parking lot. I'll be right behind them. It's not like I could lose them on the only road heading in your direction. There'll be two planes, one with the nerve gas, the other with six additional troops who are helicopter pilots."

"Okay, understood. You hang back at the top of Columbia Pass in case we have a problem here."

"Ten-four."

"That was Yancy," announced Quint, as he relayed the phone conversation to the others.

Bernice spoke up. "Quint, there is something about this whole situation that stinks."

"I know. I have the same feeling. Let's spread out and cover the storage hangar. I see headlights coming down the road."

The lights turned onto the tarmac. The team could make out the small truck piloted by Najib, followed by a twelve-seater van. Both vehicles headed right for the hangar across from the maintenance building. The team scattered around the area with good views of their quarry and close enough to tackle any problem in short order.

Not more than five minutes had elapsed after the cars disappeared into the hangar, than the drone of airplanes could be heard in the distance. It was a dark, moonless night, with little wind to cause problems for the pilots.

As the team watched the hangar from their camouflaged positions, the huge doors opened up and out of the way, allowing the three terrorists to begin setting flares along the runway to guide the pilots safely back to Planet Earth.

The lead plane was the same one they'd encountered a few days prior. The second was large, big enough to accommodate the six chopper pilots. Both landed without incident, taxied down to the end of the runway, turned around, and followed Najib back to the huge hangar, where they disappeared as the vehicles had.

Quint remarked to Jett and Jake, "No security guard?" as he headed for the only window on ground level. "These guys are unbelievable. It's like they don't give a shit if anyone knows they're here. Let's check out the window in the door and see what's up."

They managed to move up to the window without being discovered and peek in. Jake, being the tallest, had the best view. "They're all in a circle, with Najib yelling and waving his arms as usual. We should have Yancy here to tell us what he's yelling about, but I think that's his usual mode of communication. They're offloading the gas canisters, stacking them next to the C-4. Damn! If they make a mistake there'll be one hell of an explosion. I pray they don't do something dumb while we're this close."

Quint whispered, "If we knew who the others in the hotels were, we could do these fuckers now and get this finished."

Jett retorted, "Let's do these guys anyway and con-fiscate the explosives and gas."

Quint replied, "We don't know if the hotel guys already have C-4 and gas. It's a game of cat and mouse. We'll just have to wait and follow these punks back to town."

Jake said, "They're loading the gas and C-4 into the van and pickup. It must be time to distribute the goods to the hotels. They have two days until the eleventh to get the gas and C-4 in position to create their path to the virgins."

Quint called Bernice and Sue. "They're going to head out soon with the gas and explosives. You guys head back up the road and wait in the parking lot of the hotel in Jean. We'll tag along with our friends. Tell Yancy, who's waiting at Columbia Pass, to get back to the hotel, find a spot out of sight and read some lips when our friends walk through the lobby, if they stop there. If not, we'll all just fall in line and one of us will drop off with each delivery, to keep tabs on who has what."

Najib said, "Mahathir, check outside from the second-floor window. We want to be sure our infidel friends are there. The rest of you get in the van. We'll go back to the hotel at Jean, where you will find your accommodations ready. Use room service for meals. You will be taken to your helicopters at the appropriate time. Do not, I repeat, do *not* leave the rooms for any reason. Mohammed, you take the lead when we leave the hangar. Mahathir and I will be right behind you.

Take care going over the pass. You have valuable cargo. Drop the pilots off at Jean, and then we'll deliver the gas and C-4 as we go up the Strip. We'll make sure the infidels following us stay in visual contact."

Mohammed asked, "What are we going to do with the two planes and their pilots?"

Najib turned to the two fixed-wing aircraft pilots and ordered, "You two take off at daylight and fly over to Cal-Nev-Ari, familiarize yourselves with the landing strip, and then return to Mexico for another load of gas and C-4. Fill both planes so you only have to make one trip. Put all the gas and explosives in gym bags as we have here, so we can check into the hotels without much notice. Fly back to Cal-Nev-Ari and park. I'll call you when we will be there to pick up the cargo. Make a deal about landing and parking with the responsible party at the airstrip. Money talks."

Quint whispered, "The hangar doors are opening. They must be ready to head back to Jean or on to Vegas."

The van pulled out onto the tarmac, followed by the small pickup. When they had cleared them, the doors once again retreated to the closed position.

"The van is full of people, but I couldn't tell who was in it. The two planes didn't fire up. I'll check and see if the pilots are still there. They may want to wait for daylight to take off and not light up the runways again," said Jake.

"Okay, you hang here; we'll stay with the van and pickup. Give us a call when you find out anything," said Quint.

The team had to stay back a little farther than desirable because the road was lonely and it would be obvious if they stayed too close. With Yancy at the pass and the girls in Jean, they could afford to allow their quarry to be out of sight on the road.

There was only one turnoff. It headed for Good-springs and then back into Jean.

Jett called Yancy. "They're near the top of the pass. Head back down to Jean and get in position to read some lips if you can."

Yancy smiled to himself. *This is way better than being the good guy. I could never stand that patriotic bullshit. It's the same all over the word. Money talks, bullshit walks. It's nice to have a cool two million heading for my account; those dumbass terrorists were an easy mark. This is going to be interesting, to say the least. Having no conscience is the only way to fly. Nobody really gives a shit about anyone else anyway. Fuck it. Fuck 'em all!"*

"Ten-four, Jett, I'm on my way."

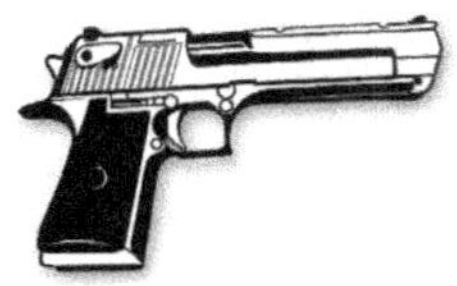

Chapter Seventeen

Distribution

Jake called from the hangar. "The pilots are still here, and it looks like they're going to spend the night. What should I do?"

"Head for Jean, we'll keep you updated as to our position," responded Quint.

Bernice reported in. "They came by the hotel and dropped off the chopper pilots. Now they're headed down the old LA highway towards town. We're on their tail. Yancy is behind us."

Quint shot back, "We have to wait for Jake. We'll catch up with you."

The first stop was the Mandalay Bay. The terrorists must have called ahead, for the vehicles drove around to the back near the convention facilities entrance and met two guys. After a short meeting, they transferred two of the bags to them.

"Bernice, you stick with these two and see if you can figure out if the bags are gas or explosives. There are red bags and green bags, and we don't know which is which."

Bernice bailed out of the car and followed the two into the back entrance of the hotel as the rest of the team tagged along with Najib, who backed out onto the Strip, heading north.

Staying close to the two terrorists was not a problem in the busy hotel. They walked through the lobby to the elevator banks. Bernice had to move in a little too close for her liking, but she needed to get on the same elevator. Lucky for her, the lift was crowded with a loud, intoxicated group of people.

The two terrorists were young and fit the profile of every terrorist around the globe, but Vegas was loaded with people from all over the world, and their English was very good, so they didn't draw any special attention. The bad guys didn't seem the least bit nervous, joking with each other and the passengers on the way up, after punching in the floor below the penthouse, where a special keycard was required to have access. They would be the last ones off the elevator. Bernice had pressed the button for the floor just below them. She exited on her floor and found the emergency stairwell, hurrying up to see what room they were in.

She pushed the emergency door open just as she heard the familiar ding as the elevator doors opened. She could see down the hallway, and lucky for her, the two scumbags had just gotten off the elevator and were walking down the hall with their backs to her. They keyed the last room on the right in the long hall and entered. She stayed back watching, hoping they wouldn't stay long and she could figure a way to get into the room to discover which device was in which bag.

To her good fortune, the two were not in the room more than a few minutes before they came back and punched in the down button. When the doors closed, she ran to see what floor they may have gotten off on. To her surprise the elevator went all the way to the casino level. That would give her time to find a way into the room.

From past experience, Bernice thought the best way into the room was to call the bell desk and say she'd locked herself out of her room.

Using the house phone at the end of the hall, she called the bell desk. The bell captain said he'd send someone right up.

It was the same in every hotel, no matter where. If you wanted something to happen, you called the bell captain, and voila!

The bellman arrived in short order and before he could ask her anything, she gave him a hundred-dollar bill, acting a little drunk in the charade to keep him from getting too nosy. He smiled and using his pass key opened the door. He departed quickly, not wanting to be alone with an intoxicated woman.

Bernice entered the room and quickly checked the bags. They contained gas canisters. Leaving the room, she called Quint, "The bags here are green, and they contain the gas canisters."

Quint said, "Okay, so the red ones are explosives. You hang out there and keep an eye on those two for now. Are they on the top floor?

"Yes, well actually one floor from the top, where the penthouses are located."

"Okay, check and see if there is access to the roof from where you are. The stairwell should go all the way up. I think they will try and put the gas in the ventilation system through the air handlers, so as to flood the whole building."

Bernice returned to the stairwell and continued up the stairs to find they led to the roof. The heating and cooling systems were there for the picking, just waiting to receive the nerve gas.

"Bingo, Quint," Bernice reported on the cell. "Easy access for them to do their dirty work."

"Bernice, stay on the roof for now. If they show up early for some reason, kill them, then take the bags down to the back entrance and give me a call."

As the team motored north on the Strip, the next stop was the Flamingo. The terrorists pulled around to the rear service dock and handed over the green gym bags to one guy. He turned and headed towards the service entrance.

Quint said, "Jake, tail this guy and give us a call."

"Okay. Can I just kill the fucker and confiscate the goods? Save us a lot of trouble."

"Come on, Jake. Just keep him in your sights. I think the cooling towers and cooling units are on the ground. Shouldn't be too tough to take him out when we need to."

Jake jumped from the car and followed their quarry into the bowels of the hotel. He was easy to follow, not even looking back to check his six.

When Mohammed pulled into the Treasure Island, Sue said, "If you don't mind, I'll take this one. I need to stretch my muscles."

It was the same routine. The van pulled around to the rear loading dock. At the end of the dock was a guy who didn't smile, wave, or acknowledge anyone as he picked up the gym bags, then turned, and almost ran back to the rear entrance.

Sue stepped out of the car and had to run to keep the scumbag in sight. He disappeared through the rear entrance door, but tripped and fell just inside the swinging doors. Sue nearly fell over him. She bent over and helped him up, trying not to give herself away. He was indignant, not wanting any help from a female.

Brushing himself off, he headed for the elevator banks, with Sue giving him plenty of room. He pressed the elevator button and when it opened, he was the only one who got on, so Sue stayed behind, but watched the floor indicator stop at the second floor.

She decided to look for the heating and cooling system and worry about him later. He would have to leave the room for chow sometime or room service would deliver and she would follow them. A C-note would get as much information as she needed.

Sue figured if his room was on the second floor, the equipment he was going to dump the gas into must be on the ground somewhere.

She headed back to the rear entrance and started walking the property. She hadn't gone far before she found the fenced-off area where the ventilation system equipment was located.

She typed in Quint's number. It rang once. "Quint here."

"Quint, the bad guy is on the second floor, and the equipment is on the street level around back. It's fenced and locked, but not a big deal to get into."

"Okay, you hang there and keep an eye on this dude." He continued, "There should only be one more to go, and that's the Sahara, unless they changed the plan."

Sure enough, the van and pickup pulled into the Sahara's Paradise Road entrance. The Sahara being one of the older hotels, Quint figured the ventilation system would be up on the top of the building.

The van and truck continued into valet parking, and money exchanged hands, allowing them to pull up to check-in, where Mohammed stepped out with two green bags and Najib joined him. Jett said, "Okay, this guy's mine."

Mohammed was met by a man who took the bags. The three then walked into the hotel and headed for the elevators.

Jett kept his distance. The elevator was crowded, so he was able to slip on with his targets.

The elevator was slow. Jett stood near the front and had to move every time the lift stopped to disembark a guest. They were near the top floor when he punched in the next to the last floor, hoping his bad guys were not getting off with him. He didn't have a key, and it would be obvious his ride was not to find a room.

To his relief, the green bag trio stayed on when he exited. Jett hurried down the hall to the emergency stairwell and climbed up to the next floor, hoping to see what room they were occupying.

He peeked out the emergency door. Finding the hall empty he ran down to the elevator and found it had gone up to the penthouse. He didn't have a key for that, so he ran back to the stairwell and up to the penthouse level, only to find the door was locked. The next level had to be the roof access, so Jett climbed up and found the roof access door unlocked. Slowly pushing the door open, he peered out to see his prey talking just out of earshot. He figured by the way they were gesturing a discussion was going on regarding where to put the gas.

It appeared a decision was made, as they headed back towards the roof access door and Jett's position.

He didn't have time to run down the stairwell out of sight, so he decided to bluff his way past them.

Jett bumped into Mohammed on purpose, excused himself, and asked, "Is there a good view of the Strip from here?"

Mohammed looked angered at the intrusion, but Najib pulled on his arm saying something in Arabic, and he settled down. They ignored him and continued through the door.

Jett was lucky they were in a hurry. He waited a few minutes and then took the elevator down to the casino floor and waited. He didn't have to wait long before Mohammed and Najib appeared. The third man, with the green bags, must have stayed up on the roof. He would be dealt with later. Jett followed Mohammed and Najib out the front door, back to check-in parking, where they got in the van and headed down East Sahara towards the Boulder Highway. Jett got on the cell. "Quint, it looks like Mohammed and Najib are heading back to the Hacienda."

"Hail a cab and stay on their tail."

"Ten-four."

It was easy to follow someone when you knew where they were going, so Jett told the cabbie to stay a number of cars behind them. Since they had seen him, it wouldn't bode well to have them get another look.

The two terrorists pulled into the Hacienda check-in parking and went up to their rooms. Jett waited downstairs and before long, Mohammed and Najib appeared with a bellman's cart loaded with stuff from their rooms. With the van loaded, they headed back towards Boulder City.

Jett kept the cabbie back a safe distance as they followed the van towards Boulder City and into the parking lot of the Railroad Pass Hotel and Casino, where Mohammed parked the van. The two men entered the casino through the rear door.

Jett stayed in the parking lot and watched the van, not wanting to get caught by accident. It wasn't long before Mohammed came out with a bellman's cart and hauled their bags into the hotel. Just as Jett was about to follow Mohammed, his cell buzzed. "Jett here."

"Jett, how is it going with Mohammed?"

"He and Najib checked out of the Hacienda and moved into the Railroad Pass."

Quint said, "I wonder what the hell is going on. We are spread pretty damn thin right now, and it doesn't look to get any better. You hang with Mohammed wherever he goes. I'll send Jesse out there to watch the rooms. Did he ever drop off any of the red bags?"

"No. The red bags are still in the van."

"Okay, you be sure and keep him in your sights."

"I can't get too close. I had a problem on the roof at the Sahara, and they've seen me."

"Shit! Okay, listen. I'm going to send Keno along with Jesse. He can help you with Mohammed and Najib, so you can stay out of sight."

"Sounds good, but you better hurry them along, he may take off any time."

"They're on the way."

Yancy called Quint. "Where do you want me to go, Quint? I'm at the end of the Strip. I was delayed in the traffic."

"Come to the safe house. I'm sending Jesse and Keno out to help Jett. We know where all the parties are with the gas, but Mohammed and Najib still have the red bags and their destination is in doubt. Keno and Jett will be following them. You can come back here and take care of the communications. I'll join Jett and Keno."

"Okay, I'm on my way."

Quint called Jett's cell again. "Jett, have you seen Mahathir?"

"No."

"Shit, I haven't either. I'll be right there. Have Jesse and Keno showed up yet?"

"No."

Quint was thinking, *If Mahathir is not in the van, where the hell is he? How could we lose track of him? Making the assumption he was in the van was not a good idea. Shit! He must have stayed behind with the fixed-wing pilots. Damn, now we have lost one very important part of the puzzle, a loose end.*

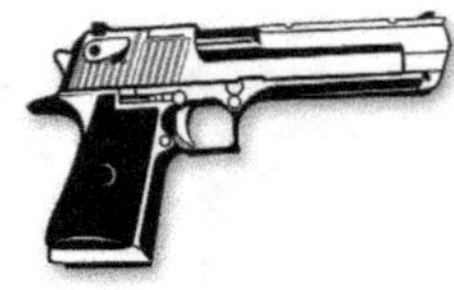

Chapter Eighteen

Red Bags

"Mahathir, where are you?' asked Najib.

"I'm at the New York-New York as you instructed."

"Okay. Do you have the bags?"

"Yes, they're in the pickup in guest parking. My room is about halfway up in the high-rise as directed. The room is facing the Strip."

"Okay, take the bags up to the room. Mohammed and I will be along in an hour or so. He'll bring the rest of the red bags. He will be followed as expected, but it won't matter. I'll have Yancy give them a false time for our little surprise. The building will come down like in New York, and the infidels will pay once again. Praise be to Allah."

When Quint got to the Railroad Pass Hotel, it was still a couple of hours before sunrise. Jesse and Keno were already there. He told Keno to head back to the safe house to relieve Yancy and tell him to come back to the Railroad Pass.

"Jett, we can't find Mahathir. Maybe Yancy can read some lips and give us a clue. I didn't think he was bright enough to be out on his own. Maybe Najib killed him!" said Quint.

"Who knows, all these fuckers are wingnuts. The van has the red bags in the back. I'll be glad when we can do them all and be done with it. They've been in the hotel a long time; maybe we should check and see what's up. I didn't follow them to their rooms. We can bribe the desk clerk to find out their room number," replied Jett.

"Okay, I'll take care of that. You stay here, out of sight. Jesse, you go and watch the rear door. They may have more than one vehicle. Shit! They may have planted a car here to throw us off. Damn!"

Quint ran into the hotel, and after finding the registration desk, he palmed a C-note into the clerk's hand and found out the room number for Najib and Mohammed.

He took the first elevator to the second floor and bribed the maid to let him check out the room. The room was empty, except for their personal bags.

Going back downstairs he walked out to the parking lot to find Jett waving at him. When he got up close enough to hear, Jett said, "Mohammed just got into the van, but I didn't see Najib."

"I think Najib already flew the coop. The room was empty except for their shaving kits. Jesse, you and I will stay here. Jett, you follow Mohammed. Tomorrow is D-Day, so we don't have much time. If Najib hasn't left, we'll see him, and if he has, we'll wait for word from you on Mohammed. They won't be far apart at this stage of the game," Quint reflected.

When Yancy was on his way out to the Railroad Pass Casino, his cell rang. "Yancy here."

"Yancy, you know who this is? Right?"

"Yes, what's up now, Najib?"

"Don't sound so enthused, Yancy. We have lots to do. Part of your money will be in the bank by morning, the rest in cash as you requested. You'll have to trust me for now."

"I don't trust you, Najib, and if you cross me I'll kill you as quickly as I would a snake. So get off all the happy talk and get to the fucking point."

"You are a typical money-hungry capitalist pig. I read you like a book. You'd kill your own mother for a buck."

"Okay, Najib, so we have similar traits. What do you want?"

"I'm heading out to Cal-Nev-Ari to pick up more C-4, and I want you to tell your cohorts we plan to do the hotels with gas at four in the morning on 9/11. Also tell them the New York-New York will go at seven, giving the others enough time to jam the Strip with emergency equipment. The confusion will make it sweet. Only thing is, we'll be doing Allah's will one hour earlier and at different locations than they know about right now. Pass that information along so they will be busy with the bogus locations and allow us to do our business without interference.

"I left one million in cash in a locker in the Union Plaza bus depot. The key will be at the front desk of the Strat in an envelope with your name on the front. It has not been a pleasure working with you lowlife infidels."

"Save the sarcasm for someone who gives a shit. You can't get to me, pal, I don't care about your world or the team's world. The only world important to me is my world. So fuck you."

Najib was thinking, *I will behead that arrogant lowlife as soon as possible.*

Yancy closed the cell as he was entering the Railroad Pass's guest parking. He found Quint and Jesse standing next to one of the many over-the-road trucks parked for the night.

"Quint, before we do anything I need to talk with you."

"Okay, Yancy, let's step over next to that cattle hauler."

"I didn't tell you all that Najib said earlier because I wasn't sure I read him right. But the more I think about it, I believe my reading was correct."

"Okay, Yancy, get on with it. What did he say?"

"Well, you're not going to like it for sure."

"Okay, again. Now spit it out."

"They're going to dump the gas at four in the morning on 9/11. Then, when all the confusion is at its peak, they will set off the C-4 at the New York-New York. He didn't mention the helicopters. I don't know about them."

"Did he say if all the players were in the game, or are there more coming? Some we don't know about?"

"You know as much as I do now; he didn't mention any more players or equipment. Sorry I didn't tell you earlier, but I wasn't sure."

"What changed your mind?"

"It was when you called and said he'd moved to the Railroad Pass. I don't think he intends to see the Vestal Virgins with the rest of the psychopaths. He's planning his escape, getting closer to wherever it is he's going. He'll probably give out his instructions by phone and be long gone when the shit hits the fan."

"You're reading a lot into his motives."

"I think I'm right. I know his type, having been there myself at one time in my life. He's not going to kill himself. He doesn't believe in the Allah bullshit any more than I do.

"He's money hungry, same as most of the world's zealots. The asshole is no better than a traveling tent evangelist sucking all the blood and money he can out of the suckers under his canopy before taking a powder."

"Okay, we'll hang out here. You know we've lost Mahathir, and now Najib. We may have to go ahead and take out all the bad guys we know about, and hope we've got them all."

Yancy added, "You know, I do remember Najib saying something about Cal-Nev-Ari. It didn't fit into any of the conversations I witnessed. Maybe he's planning on taking his leave from there?"

"That could be. It's out of the way and little known to those not from around here. He would have to have a plane to leave from there. Perhaps those fixed-wing guys have something to do with his escape plans. Maybe you should take a ride out there and see if he's around. I believe it's about twenty miles past Searchlight on the way to Needles."

"Yeah, I know where it is."

"Okay, take a ride over there and keep me posted."

Yancy returned to his car. *Damn, these guys are easy. Not a sign of suspicion from Quint or any of the team. I may just kill that fuck Najib, take the money, and haul ass out of town. Let all the shit go down as it will. Why should I give a damn, both are terrorists in the mind of the others.*

As Yancy's car left the parking lot, Quint was not at all pleased with the present situation. He didn't want to dilly-dally any longer and blow the mission, trying to be too cute.

As Quint turned to Jesse, his cell rang. "Quint here. What's up, Bernice?"

"We have a problem here at the Bay. I think I may have blown this part of the mission, maybe let the cat out of the bag for the whole show!"

"Jesus, Bernice, slow down and fill me in."

Quint put his cell on the speaker, so Jesse could hear Bernice's situation.

"Well, it was kind of my mistake but then again, not all my fault. I was hanging out on the roof near the ventilation system when some nerd and his girlfriend got up here somehow to check out the view.

"They began to make whoopie near the edge. When it got hot and heavy, our two terrorists showed up with their little green bags. The couple playing near the edge didn't want any company and headed for the exit to go back downstairs. Well, the scumbags panicked, thinking they had to do something with the couple so they wouldn't interfere with their plot. I thought they were going to kill them, so I stepped in with all the force I could muster.

"While I was busy trying to save the couple, they escaped, leaving me with two very pissed-off terrorists. I tried to kill them without shooting, using my knife. The fight was short, but not without some blood on both sides. They were well-trained in some sort of martial arts I have not encountered before. In order to save my own ass, I had to shoot them, making a considerable amount of noise. This all happened about five minutes ago. My arm and leg have knife wounds, along with my right hand. I have stopped the bleeding, but I would appreciate it if you could get up here and help me with the bodies. What the hell should I do with them for now?"

"Okay. Listen. We'll be there in thirty minutes. Hide the bags in case security comes up. The couple may have run down to the casino and reported being attacked. If we're lucky they may not want to be further involved. If security shows up, use your private investigator ID to stall them. Jesse and I are on the road."

"Okay, will do. You might break the speed limit on your way. I have lost some blood and feel lightheaded."

Shit! What else can go wrong? That fucking Murphy is about to have a cloudburst on our parade. "Pedal to the metal, Jesse!"

Jesse figured the fastest way from the check-in lane to the hotel front door was a twenty dollar bill to the valet parking attendant. It worked just fine, for they were on their way to the roof in no time.

"There she is, Jesse," said Quint. "Damn, this must have been some fight. She looks dead."

Quint bent down and felt for Bernice's pulse. "She has a good pulse. I think she just passed out from loss of blood. We need to get her somewhere on the double. Let's drag the two stiffs behind the air equipment and leave them. Make sure we get all their IDs, and later on we can call and leave an anonymous tip. Find the gas bags, take them with you and bring the car around to the rear. I'll bring her down. She is semiconscious and can help me. I'll grab some towels in the hallway to cover her wounds. She'll appear to be a happy camper full of free slot drinks."

With Bernice in the car, Jesse headed north on the Strip to Tropicana, where he turned east to Maryland Parkway. From there it was on to Desert Inn Road and Sunrise Hospital's emergency room.

Quint flashed their ID cards and told the emergency people that Bernice was on a government Special Operations mission. He said they would have normally taken her to Nellis Air Force Base, but thought her condition needed immediate attention. He added that there was no need to report her status to the local authorities, because the mission was top secret. The emergency people were convinced and willing to do their part in the service of their country.

Bernice didn't want to stay in the hospital, but it would take her some time to recover, so Quint told her to stay put until she felt strong enough to get back in the game and then call the safe house for Keno to pick her up.

"We have to get back out to Railroad Pass," Quint said, as they left her room.

When Yancy arrived at Cal-Nev-Ari, he drove past the restaurant toward the runway, looking for Najib's vehicle. It was near daylight and there was little movement in the small airport community.

He spotted the van without any trouble. It was parked by the two small planes that had been out in Sandy Valley. They were loading bags into the van as he pulled up.

Najib looked up. He was not smiling. "What the hell are you doing here? You're supposed to be giving your cohorts all the phony information."

"Don't get excited, Najib. I'm taking care of my end. They are suspicious about your whereabouts, so I told them I might be able to find you. They are also concerned that Mahathir is also missing. I think they may just kill all the guys you have planted so far and then be on the hunt for you and dimwit Mahathir."

"You, Yancy, are the dimwit. Mahathir is going to be praised by Allah for his sacrifice. You will die for nothing. I would like to kill you myself, but I have a considerable amount of money invested, and your job is not finished. Now go back and tell them the plan is on schedule, that we will put the gas into the ventilation systems at four in the morning, and the New York-New York will go up at seven.

"It doesn't matter if they kill my people before that, for I have changed the plan. The van here will be driven into the New York-New York at the same time that Mahathir sets off his C-4, and the helicopters will hit downtown a few minutes before. You tell them the choppers won't be used, so they won't watch the hotel in Jean for the pilots or the chopper agency. You can also tell them that I've taken off in one of the small planes heading south."

"Who's driving the van into the New York-New York?"

"One of the pilots here requested that honor. I have obliged him."

"So you lowlife cockroach will just stand by and watch your fellow wingnuts find the virgins, while you move on with a pocketful of money and your ass in one piece!"

"Someone has to direct the war. Now get back to town and earn the blood money you have taken from me."

Yancy got back into his car and headed back to the Railroad Pass Hotel.

Quint and Jesse returned to the Railroad Pass Hotel hoping to find Yancy back and some news of Najib, but he hadn't returned yet. Quint was pondering if he should make his move and take out everyone they knew about and hope to find Najib and his dimwitted partner before they could do any damage. If Yancy was correct, Najib wasn't about to commit his soul to Allah, but was still dangerous with enough knowledge to use a cellphone to set off a vest he'd talked Mahathir into wearing, pulling the trigger as Mahathir walked into a hotel lobby.

While they were watching cars pull onto the property from the Boulder Highway, Quint's cell rang. It was Jett.

Jett spoke softly. "I'm standing in valet parking at the New York-New York. I followed Mohammed here, but I got caught in a traffic jam between two dimbulb cab drivers fighting over who was next in line, and I lost him. He's in the hotel somewhere, because his van in parked in valet. The truck is here too, so Mahathir must be here. The red bags are not in it or the truck. He must have taken them into the hotel. It's a big place, and finding them would be impossible without evacuating the whole place."

"Damn! That Murphy is working overtime. Shit. I think we'll have to hold off for now. If we go to the local authorities, the biggest panic button in the world will be pressed. We might be able to take the necessary action to defuse the terrorists' threat if we are patient. From what Yancy was able to pick up, they're planning their first move for tomorrow morning, so we have a few hours to work with. I want to find Najib before we begin the elimination of his team. He will show up for the kill, but not be a hands-on executioner. He's a coward and money hungry. We can wait him out."

"So, what do you want me to do?"

"Stay put, and watch Mohammed's vehicle. He doesn't look like the type to seek the virgins. I'm sure he'll return before Mahathir blows himself up. You take him down and do whatever it takes to find out their room number. Then we'll deal with Mahathir."

"Okay, but I could check with the bell captain for more information."

Quint was a little testy with his response, "I'll bet they've been around long enough to have covered those bases by now. You watch for him; we are going hunting for Najib."

Yancy returned to the Railroad Pass Hotel to find Quint watching the front entrance from the guest parking lot.

"Quint, I found Najib, and he won't be coming back to town. He's taking one of the small planes that was out in Sandy Valley and will give the signal to set off the fireworks from a safe distance. I told you he was a cowardly, money-hungry piece of shit. I was sitting in the restaurant in Cal-Nev-Ari while he was chatting with his pilots over dinner. There is a partition between the cafe and the bar. He didn't have a clue I was there. He will set the terror in motion with a conference call; they will all get the message at the same time. The gas goes first and then the New York-New York," explained Yancy.

"Thanks, Yancy. We know about the New York-New York after following Mohammed to the hotel with the extra C-4. You are sure we know about all the players?"

"Yes. He didn't mention any more, but he did say the chopper pilots were not going to hijack the helicopters. The pilots are going to assist with the gas. He thought it would screw things up if the choppers had a problem. I also thought hijacking the helicopters was a bit too ambitious. Anyway, that's all I found out. What do you want me to do now?"

Chapter Nineteen

It was all Jett could do to control himself and not kill the terrorist before he got all the information he could out of him to keep from causing a stampede in the city.

While he was pondering the situation, he watched Mohammed giving his claim check to the valet booth. He didn't appear to be in a hurry or show any signs of someone about to participate in the murder of hundreds, if not thousands, of innocent people, along with the destruction of a world-class hotel.

Some currency passed from Mohammed to the valet booth guy, and his keys were handed over. The van was in the parking area saved for customers who came up with some front money to keep their vehicle close at hand.

Jett slipped into the shotgun side of the van, just as Mohammed was inserting the key to start the engine. Mohammed was surprised to find himself looking into the barrel of a WWI era Colt .45.

The handgun's power was not lost on Mohammed, who let the key go and put both hands on the wheel. Jett said, "Be a good fellow and start the engine. We're going for a little ride. If anything doesn't go my way, you will die with a bullet to your head, in which case you will not have poems written about your sacrifice for Allah. Now ease out of the parking area and take a left on Tropicana and a left on the Strip. When you get to St. Louis make a right."

When they pulled up to the safe house, Keno came out to give Jett a hand and said, "I just returned from picking up Bernice. She is still weak but back in the world. What have you in mind for this piece of shit?"

"He's going to reveal the room number where the C-4 is in the hotel. Then we are going to take down Mahathir and defuse a very touchy situation without disturbing the guests or creating widespread panic."

Mohammed, who understood the situation and the chatter, didn't show any fear or emotion of any kind. He apparently had resigned himself to the coming torture and probable death.

When they brought him inside, Bernice took one look and decided she wanted to help get the information out of the scumbag. She said, "If I can be of any assistance, please allow me."

Jett gave Quint a call. "Quint, we have Mohammed at the safe house."

"Good work, Jett. We'll be there in a few minutes. Yancy just gave us the latest on Najib. We may not be able to kill the coward. He's going to head south via the plane from Sandy Valley. He plans to coordinate the attack by conference call early tomorrow morning. But we'll be able to take down everyone before he gives the word. We don't have much time to work on Mohammed."

"Okay, we'll get started with the interview," replied Jett.

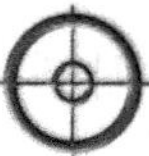

After the van was loaded, Najib and the volunteer pilot got into the vehicle for their trek to Vegas. He told the other pilot to wait for his return sometime after daylight on the eleventh, just a few hours away. They would have just enough time to drive to town and coordinate with Mahathir on the timing to pull the trigger on the C-4 and crash the van into the rear entrance of the hotel.

Najib got on his cell to call the lead helicopter pilot at the hotel in Jean. They agreed on five rings to signal it was time to receive the final orders.

"Najib here. You will follow the plan I gave you when we first met. The vehicle you will use is in guest parking. The key to the van is at the registration desk. Ask the clerk for the envelope with Mar Tar written on it. Go to the desk alone. At no time should you all be together in a group. Go out to the van one at a time. It's a red van with Arizona license plates.

After you take over the helicopter tour building at eleven-thirty tonight, you will hit the downtown hotels just before midnight. There are numerous targets of opportunity to choose from. We'll hit the New York-New York at midnight. In the name of Allah we will all become martyrs and be remembered as striking one of the biggest blows in the world against the infidels. Praise be to God."

The fixed-wing pilot turned the van toward town. Their destiny with a glorious death was near. Najib neglected to tell the pilot that when he drove the truck into the hotel he would be alone. Najib and the other pilot would be on their way to South America with enough cash to last a lifetime, and maybe plan another blow against the infidels.

When Yancy, Quint, and Jesse arrived, Bernice, Jett, and Keno were having a discussion about what type of torture might get Mohammed to spill the beans on his cohorts.

Quint stepped in and said, "We'll start with just asking him. He knows he's going to die if he doesn't give it up, but he wants to die a hero in the eyes of his fellow wingnuts, so he might not want to die in this house without any recognition. Then again, he might not want to die at all, like his partner Najib. We'll see."

Quint sat down in a chair facing Mohammed and asked him, "What room is Mahathir in?"

Mohammed didn't respond.

Quint repeated, "What room is Mahathir in? You might not want to test the limits of your pain tolerance. Just give us the number."

With a voice steeped in sarcasm, Mohammed responded, "You capitalist greedy pigs should be able to figure it out. It's simple enough. You will not get any information from me. I willingly die for my

220

beliefs. What will you die for? Allah has plans for the world that have covered a thousand years. How long have you been around—say three hundred or so years? We will dominate the world in the end. All your false religious prophecies and superficial economic ideas will just be added to the dustbin of history. So, as you say in the West, fuck off.'"

Jett said, "Mohammed, it will be a pleasure to help you die for Allah. I will make it a slow process, so you can keep giving of yourself."

Quint interjected. "We're running out of time. Let's get on with it. We'll start with waterboarding and if that doesn't loosen his tongue, we can test his endurance for pain."

Yancy was thinking, *This is not going in a good direction. Najib may have told Mohammed about the deal I made with him, and things could get sticky. I need to figure out a way to shut Mohammed up. Damn!*

Yancy spoke up. "Let's take his DNA and kill his whole family, following the tree as far back as we can, if he doesn't give up the room number."

Mohammed perked up when he heard Yancy's suggestion. "I don't have any family. They were all killed in the Iraq-Iran war. Your atempt to intimidate me with family is useless."

Quint said, "Let's get on with the waterboarding."

"How many times is that, Jett?" asked Quint.

"I think that's number ten. He doesn't give a shit whether he lives or dies. How do we terrorize a terrorist?"

Yancy spoke up again. "How about we just kill the fucker and pull the fire alarms in the hotel?"

"Good thought, except if Mahathir hears the alarms going off, he will pull the trigger on the C-4," replied Jett. "I think we should keep the waterboarding going. He'll crack sooner or later."

Yancy suggested, "How about I go back to the hotel and roam the halls. Who knows, I might stumble onto the right floor and room. If he cracks in the meantime, you can call, and I'll be there ready to act."

Bernice said, "While you're there, check who has been ordering room service enough times to suggest they haven't left their room."

"Good suggestion, Bernice," said Quint.

Yancy left the safe house and climbed into his car. *Damn, I was lucky to get out of there. I think Mohammed is on his last leg of resistance. He might just spill more than what the room number is.*

He didn't have a plan of action, but he knew it was time to get out of Dodge. His cell barked, "Yancy here."

"Meet me in the parking garage at the New York-New York, fifth floor. I have some cash for you. It entails a small detail we neglected before," said Najib.

"Fuck you, I'm not doing anymore. I'm on my way out of town."

"Will one million in cash change your mind?"

"You might get my attention with that."

I'll meet with this asshole one more time, but it will be the last. I think I'll kill the fucker and make the world a safer place.

"Okay, you've pulled my chain. I'll see you there, in twenty minutes!"

Quint called a meeting while they gave Mohammed a few minutes to consider his future.

"I think we should call Jake and Sue. It's time to eliminate the gas guys. Keno, you go and give Sue a hand at the Treasure Island. Jesse, you head over to the Flamingo and help Jake take out his target.

When you and Jake finish there, head over to the Sahara and take care of that problem. Then all we have to worry about is the New York-New York. You guys take off, and I'll give them a call to let them know you're on the way. Let's do it," said Quint.

When Sue got the call from Quint, she left her post watching the ventilation system for any attempt to release the gas in the air handler and hurried around to valet parking to wait for Keno. Her quarry was safely in his room for now.

Keno dropped a fin on the valet parking guy to keep his car handy. He said there would be another fin on the way out. The valet guy smiled and left the car where Keno had parked it.

Looking around he saw Sue wave at him to join her at the front door.

"Hello, Sue. Do we know where our bad guy is?"

"Yes, he's in a room on the second floor—number 2002 just down from the elevator. He's a paranoid basket case. I don't think he's all in for a trip to meet the virgins. All he is supposed to do is release the gas and disappear. We'll help him with the disappearing part. I've been out of the loop. What's up with the rest of the team?"

"It's a long story. I'll fill you in after we do this scumbag."

"Okay, let's head up to his room and help him on his journey."

When they got off the elevator, the hallway was empty except for a housekeeping cart loaded with supplies and linen for the rooms that were being cleaned. All maid service in the evening was special request, like late check-outs or room changes that needed a touch up.

The cart was in front of room 2002, and when they walked by, the room looked empty except for the maid. Keno pulled a sawbuck out of his folding money and slipped it into the maid's hand. "Where is the guy who was in this room?"

She smiled as the ten-spot disappeared into her apron pocket. "He checked out about five minutes ago."

"Jesus," Sue gasped. She turned to find the stairs, not wanting to wait for the elevator, and with Keno hot on her heels, hurried back down to the cooling towers.

As they turned the corner of the hotel's backside, they saw no activity around the ventilation system. Keno said, "He must have panicked; they are not scheduled to release the gas until eleven. I wonder where he is now?"

"You don't need to wonder—there he is at the end of the building. He's carrying the green bag," responded Sue. "Should we shoot him or try and take him down?"

"I don't know. You're the terror expert," said Keno.

"Well, we don't have time to draw straws. I'll get his attention and you tackle him from the rear. He might have some information that will help us."

Sue ran to the fencing that surrounded the equipment, yelling at the terrorist to drop the bag.

Keno was nearly in position to take him out when he bolted, dropping the bag in the cooling tower. He tripped on some replacement fencing and fell flat on his face. Keno kneeled down and put the small, but powerful .380 in his ear. "Do you speak English?"

The guy was in full panic mode, shaking so bad he couldn't talk. He nodded.

While Keno was taking down their quarry, Sue fished the green bag out of the vent on the cooling tower, expelling a deep breath when she found that he'd forgotten to pull the plug on the canister to release the gas. It would have had little effect in the cooling tower anyway.

She took the bag over to where Keno had their bad guy sitting with his hands zip tied behind his back. "I'll call Quint and see what they want to do with this asshole. Has he had anything to say?"

"Yeah, he was doing this job for the money. He's not a fanatic. He doesn't know what's in the bag or care about anything but the money he was supposed to get later this evening. Dumbshit thought someone was going to stick around and pay him. He's on the edge of losing it altogether and doesn't know anything about the rest of the group. Like one hand doesn't know what the other hand is doing. If it were up to me, I'd let him go."

Sue called Quint and gave him a report on their situation. He agreed with Keno, not wanting to have another body to worry about. The guy didn't have the resources to do anything more. "Let him go, and head over to the New York-New York. Yancy is over there roaming the halls, hoping to get lucky and find Mahathir. Keno can fill you in on the situation."

"Okay, we'll let him go and get over there."

"Let him go, Keno," said Sue, "but first take all his ID and money. He'll have nothing to do any harm with."

The guy was bowing and scraping, showing his gratitude, but he didn't turn and run, he walked backwards until he was around the corner and out of sight.

They ran back over to valet parking, jumped into Keno's car, and raced out of the parking lot, heading for the showdown at the New York-New York.

Jake got the call from Quint, letting him know that Jesse was on his way to help him take out the bad guy with the gas. He walked around to the front of the hotel just in time to see Jesse pull into the hotel check-in parking area. He left the key in the limo, yelling at the door man he'd be out in a few and would take care of things then. The doorman nodded in his direction and went on with the traffic jam he was trying to control.

Jesse looked around and saw Jake waving to get his attention. When they were close enough to talk, Jake said, "Our guy is on the ninth floor in the eleventh room down the hall. He hasn't left the room for the past twelve hours. He's a serious-looking dude and may be hard to handle. We need to surprise him without making a scene and causing the hotel to go into panic mode. So far I haven't alerted security or the local authorities. I just talked to Quint, and we're good so far. He's sure this guy doesn't know about Mahathir or the New York-New York. He won't be able to give us anything new, so if he gets a ticket to visit the virgins, if won't be a big loss on our end."

"Okay, so how do you want to do this?"

"I've been thinking about that, and room service could be our answer. He's been using them every few hours for fruit, nuts, and salads. A call to room service, if he's on schedule, should be made any time now. We'll intercept the room service waiter, give him a couple of C-notes and viola! We're in the room."

"What if the room service guy doesn't want to cooperate?"

"Never heard of one who would turn down a couple of hundred bucks."

They waited on the room service guy for twenty minutes, and when he didn't show, Jake said, "Well, I guess he's not hungry. We'll have to bust into the room and hope he's not a good shot."

Jesse suggested, "Why don't we knock on the door and announce that we're room service?"

"It has a peephole."

"That's okay, we'll know he's at the door, so we bust in and knock him on his ass!"

"Never mind, here comes room service. He's pushing one of those tables set up for dinner."

Jake approached the waiter and flashed two one hundred dollar bills, "Our friend in the room you're delivering to thinks we won't be in town until tomorrow, and we want to surprise him. What do you say we roll in the table while you take a powder?"

The waiter was smiling big time as he slipped the two bills into his vest pocket. He walked back down the hall to the elevator, yelling back, "Don't forget to have him sign the check with a good size gratuity on it."

Jesse commented, "That's Vegas for you. Such humility. Greedy little fucker."

Jake knocked on the door, calling out *"ROOM SERVICE"* in a loud voice.

Jesse put his hand over the peephole as Jake prepared to shove the dinner table into the room.

There was no answer. Jake knocked harder, making his announcement again. Still no answer.

"Damn, we should have gotten a passkey from the room service guy." said Jessie. "Maybe we can find a maid and drop another hundred, rather than kicking down the door."

"Wait, I hear movement," said Jake, adding, "We should have checked the table more closely; it's set up for two. Our friend must have a guest. This may create some problems. Shit, what do we do with the woman or man, whichever is his preference, after we kill him?"

When they heard the deadbolt slide and the safety latch flip off, Jake made ready to push the room service table as forcibly as he could into the room.

As the door knob turned, Jake shoved the table into the door as hard and fast as possible, knocking down a woman clad only in a teddy. She cried out in surprise.

Jesse followed Jake and the table into the room, as their quarry ran over the woman, trying to get past them into the hall.

Jake tackled the man, who was wielding a large knife and slashed at Jake's rib cage, drawing blood. It wasn't a deep wound, and Jake grabbed his wrist and managed to twist it enough to make him drop the blade, just as Jesse hit him over the head with a dinner plate loaded with a steak, baked potato, and green veggies. He was out cold lying on the floor, but during the struggle the knife had found its way into the woman.

In a whisper, Jake said, "Shit! What the fuck do we do now? The woman looks dead, and he's not in good shape either. Look around for the green bag, and we'll get the hell out of here. We can lay the bodies next to each other like it was a domestic dispute or a hooker-john party gone bad. By the time he wakes up, it will be his problem to explain the situation. Looks like he was not all in on the religious thing."

Jesse searched the room and found the gas bags in the bathtub. As he came back into the bedroom, their terrorist started to stir.

"Damn, he's coming around," said Jake.

"Okay, we have a situation here that we can fix. Let's throw him out the window, and it will look like a murder suicide. Happens all the time here. This asshole was going to kill a hotel full of people without remorse."

Jake said, "The windows are blocked for just that reason."

230

While they were discussing their options, the man sat up. There was fear in his eyes as he looked at the dead woman and the two intruders who had taken him down.

Jake looked at him and asked, "Do you speak English?"

He nodded in the affirmative.

Jake said, "If you cooperate you will not die. We found the gas and know what you were up to. What time were you supposed to release the gas?"

"Eleven."

"Were you to call or let anyone know if you succeeded?"

"No."

"Are you being paid for this or is it your contribution to the cause?"

"Paid."

"How do you collect your money?"

"Half was up front in cash and the rest delivered by hand at the Strat, while the Strip is in turmoil."

Jesse interjected, "Let's tie him up in the bathroom, and get the hell out of here. Let him explain what went on here."

"Sounds good," Jake, agreed.

They tied the guy up in the bathroom, and leaving the woman on the floor, they took the bags and made their way down to the car.

Jake said, "When we get to the safe house we'll call security at the hotel and tell them a woman has been stabbed."

Jesse called Quint. "We have the gas. There was a little altercation in the process, but it's all taken care of."

Quint said, "Okay, we haven't found Mahathir's room number yet. We'll have to decide pretty soon what we're going to do. There's not much time left. You guys head over to the New York-New York. Call me when you get there."

"Ten-four," responded Jesse.

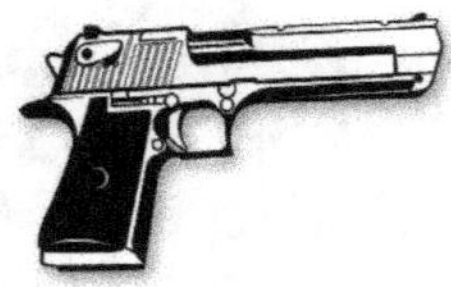

Chapter Twenty

Money or Honor

Quint had to make a decision soon, whether to alert hotel security and the local authorities or take the entire team into the New York-New York and find Mahathir. Either action would put the entire hotel in jeopardy. Panic on the Las Vegas Strip would follow.

Quint said, "We'll give waterboarding one more try and if he doesn't crack, we'll use some intimate torture." He took his cell out of his pocket and went into the other room.

Jett was setting up Mohammed for the next pour when he rolled off the table, pulling Bernice down with him. He had somehow wiggled his way out of the wrist ties. He grabbed Bernice's pistol and held it to her head.

Jett said, "If you harm her in any way, you are a dead man without the fanfare of dying in the name of Allah."

"You fucking infidels don't have a clue about dying or living for something more than money. I'm going to shoot her in the head and before you can draw your gun, I will shoot you. The waterboarding is for amateurs. Anybody can withstand that torture with a little training. You have another choice to save yourself and the woman."

Jett was trying to figure a way to signal Quint, who was in the other room on the cell, trying to check in with the team at the New York-New York.

"What are the choices you have decided I have, other than killing you?"

"Just one: release me."

"No chance of that happening."

"Your choice, infidel," Mohammed said as he pressed the pistol to Bernice's head.

Jett was about to lunge over the table and grab the handgun in a desperate attempt to save Bernice, when the sound of a Colt .45 stunned his hearing. The round passed very close to his left ear as it found its way to the forehead of Mohammed, knocking him into the wall as the pistol aimed at Bernice went off into the ceiling.

"Jesus Christ, Quint, you could have shot him from a different angle. You've made sure I won't be able to hear for a week."

"Shit, that was the least of my worries. I was right on target, and just in time, I might add. And our source of information is on his way to the happy hunting grounds. What the hell happened?"

"The son of a bitch was playing us the whole time, and when he thought he could make a move on us he did," responded Bernice.

"Well, we don't have time now to alert the hotel for evacuation."

Bernice said, "You remember when he said we could figure it out, that it was easy? What the hell was he talking about? Let's put our heads together and come up with his easy solution."

Yancy could see Najib's van parked near the elevator of the fifth floor parking garage, and he wished he'd parked further into the garage so their meeting wouldn't have so many eyes. Najib had chosen his spot well.

He parked his car near the end of the fifth floor on the opposite side, not wanting Najib to see him approach.

Coming up from the passenger side of the vehicle, Yancy, using his .38 Special revolver, knocked on the window, which was half down.

Najib, not usually caught unawares, was startled to see Yancy standing with his gun pointed at him.

"Relax, Yancy. I'm here to make you even richer than you are. Easy money for a greedy fellow like you."

Najib reached over and unlocked the door, motioning Yancy to get in. "Have a seat."

Yancy, keeping the gun pointed in Najib's direction, slid in. "You keep your hands on the wheel, asshole. Where's the cool million in cash you promised me for performing your afterthought detail?"

"You money-hungry infidels think ahead about as far as you can spit. I don't have the cash here so you can kill me and take a walk. There is a key to a locker at the Union Plaza Greyhound bus depot. In the locker is your payment for services rendered, and enough C-4 to cause considerable damage to the hotel. The bundle of cash is sitting on a pressure-sensitive release valve that will start a timer that will give you twenty minutes to collect the bundle and leave the depot."

"How do I know you haven't rigged the C-4 to go off when I lift the bundle?"

"You'll see the timer underneath. You can hold the valve down if you want, but then you'll have to stay there, or you can release it and take your chances. You're a greedy gambler, a risk taker. Let's see how bad you want the money. I'm betting you are so weak in character that you won't think about it for a minute. You'll take the money. I'm counting on your weakness to destroy the bus depot and most of the hotel. I'll be busy in the meantime. You will do all this at midnight.

"The hotel here will go up at the same time as the Plaza, and the helicopters will hit just minutes before that. It will be a beautiful blow against the evil capitalist pigs in the whore city of Las Vegas. If you don't take my offer, there is another locker with a second stash of C-4 set to go off at 12:10. So, you can take the money or you can watch it go up in smoke. It's all set, with no way to stop the process."

Yancy didn't want to kill him before he got the locker number, thinking, *This son of a bitch has connected his attack to 9/11 in his every move, sick fuck that he is. I bet it will be locker number nine or eleven. Damn, there goes that little voice again. Jesus, I thought I'd buried him so deep he would never see the light of day. Shit! He's tugging at my cape again. This can't*

236

be happening to me. I don't give a shit about anything or anybody but myself and money. It's so much easier being selfish and not caring about anything. Najib has read me pretty good, but I might surprise him with a very short retreat back into having a conscience, just long enough to kill him and give Quint a call.

"Yeah, you've pegged me because you're just as greedy as I am. I'll take the challenge of getting the cash from the bus depot and then let the place go up in smoke. Everyone in there is a sinner in the eyes of your God and mine."

"I don't like your sarcasm. I'll be glad when you make a mistake and blow yourself up. My only regret is that you will not live to see the real destruction. Like the destruction of the dam, releasing a flood over the crops that feed the nation…"

Yancy pointed the gun at Najib's head.

Najib laughed and said, "You don't have the balls to kill me. Everything I just said may be a lie. Whatever you decide to do, the process of destruction cannot be changed or stopped."

Yancy pulled the trigger on the .38 Special, striking Najib in the left shoulder. Pulling the trigger a second time sent a bullet into the right shoulder. Najib stared at him, wide eyed, not believing Yancy had the balls to shoot him, thinking he would want him alive in case the money wasn't there, thinking that Yancy would be back to collect, but he, Najib, would be gone. He slumped over, with his head on the dash, mumbling something that Yancy thought might be his last prayers to Allah. Yancy shot him again, this time in the back of the head. Searching the body, he found a key with the number 9 on it.

Leaving Najib's body in the truck, he ran over to his car and took the short trip downtown to the Plaza bus depot to collect his fee. There was not much time before the scheduled destruction would begin. Yancy typed in Quint's number.

"Quint here. What's up Yancy? Did you find the shitbird's room?"

"No, but I have good news. I ran into Najib, and he's on his way to meet the virgins."

"Shit, we didn't get the room number out of Mohammed before he expired, and now you've killed the only guy left who knows the room number. Shit, Yancy," said Quint.

"Sorry, but it became necessary to take him down. I'm on my way out of town and wanted to warn you that the helicopters are back in the equation. They are scheduled to hit downtown at a quarter to twelve, and there are some explosives in the Greyhound depot in locker number nine, and another locker is loaded also, but I don't know the number. The New York-New York will go up at midnight.

"I extracted a lot of information from a terrorist, for a novice. Be happy with that. So long, Quint. It's been fun working with you."

The cell went blank. "Jesus," said Quint to Jett. "Yancy gave us all the information we need except the room number for Mahathir. He killed Najib and is heading for parts unknown. You call Sue and Keno, and tell them to head for the chopper tour place at the south end of the strip and see if they can stop the takeover there. I'll call Jesse and Jake and have them head for the Plaza's Greyhound bus depot. We have about an hour to get all this under control. Bernice, you, Jett, and I will go to the New York-New York and begin to roam the halls. When we get there, you check with room service about any rooms using their service more than usual."

Sue explained to Keno the phone call from Jett. "We'd better get out to the helicopter tour place on the double. We don't have much time."

The Strip was unusually busy, so Keno took the freeway down to Russell and over to the Strip. Heading north on the Strip, they found the helicopter tour building parking lot full of vans used to pick up the patrons. There was one exception, a red van that didn't fit in. Sue said, "That red van must be the one the pilots used to get here from Jean. Damn!"

The building was dark, but the sound of engines being fired up could be heard. Keno said, "Guess we'll have to break in and try to stop them somehow."

"Why don't we try the door first? Maybe in their haste they didn't lock it, and we can enter without warning them."

Keno pushed on the door, and it swung open.

Sue whispered, "I don't know how to stop a helicopter while it's on the ground or in the sky, short of an RPG."

Keno whispered back, "Let's charge through the rear doors to the chopper pads firing our weapons and hope we hit something important, or at least kill the pilots before they lift off."

As they peered through the rear glass doors, it was obvious that the choppers were all in the process of getting started, with one's blades already spinning.

"We'd better take our chances right now, Sue," said Keno.

"Okay, on three we'll hit the doors and shoot as many rounds as we can at the bubbles, hoping to hit the pilots."

"One, two, three," counted Keno, and they hit the doors with pistols firing. The noise of the plexiglass popping was a good sound. There was no return fire. The pilots had been busy trying to get the choppers started, and the surprise attack left four of the helicopters grounded. Two managed to get airborne and headed toward downtown. By the time the smoke settled, there were sirens heading their way, so they didn't stick around to see if any of the pilots were alive. It would be difficult to explain what the hell they were doing there to the Metro Police Department.

As they left the parking lot, Sue got on the cell. "Quint, we stopped all but two helicopters, which are heading downtown. The cops are on the way, so we left the scene."

"Okay Sue; you guys go back to the New York-New York."

Jake walked into the bus depot in time to see Yancy standing in front of a locker. He looked like he was trying to get something out of it. He poked Jesse and pointed at Yancy. "I wonder what the hell he's doing?"

"He must trying to figure a way to get the C-4 out of the locker. Quint said he was on his way out of town. Looks like he changed his mind."

They walked up behind Yancy. Jake said, "What's up, Yancy?"

Yancy didn't give them an answer, but just kept working in the storage locker.

"Yancy, what the fuck are you doing?"

"Relax, I'll be finished in a minute. When I turn around you'll have twenty minutes to get the hell out of here or take the bundle in here outside to the railroad tracks where it won't cause too much damage, maybe not kill anyone. I'm taking the gym bag sitting here and going my own way. I'm having a short burst of conscience that will be over when I free the bag. If you want to be the heroes here, take the C-4 to the tracks. There is another locker here somewhere with C-4 in it, and I'm guessing it's in locker eleven two doors down. It would fit in with Najib's pattern of modeling everything on the original event in New York."

"Guess we could be checking locker eleven while he's working on number nine, Jake," suggested Jesse.

Jake pulled the Ka-Bar that he carried in a scabbard on the middle of his back and began to pry on locker number eleven. It was not much of challenge and opened with little effort. "Jesus," cried out Jake. "There's a huge bundle of C-4 with a timer on it, and it's ticking. I can't see the clock, but we can remove the device. It doesn't look like there's a pressure release on it."

As Jesse held out his hands to receive the bundle from Jake, Yancy said, "Well, gentlemen, I have what I want. You have twenty minutes to dispose of these devices. I suggest you get on with the program. My best wishes to you."

He took the gym bag from the locker and headed out the side door of the bus depot. *Boy, it feels good to be back on the dark side. All that goody-goody shit is a pain in the ass. It can get you killed. Let those dumbasses take their chances with the C-4. I'll just mosey out to Cal-Nev-Ari, bribe the pilot with a little cash to sell me his plane, and I'm off to Belize. Life is good.*

Jesse grabbed the stack of explosives in locker eleven and made for the rear entrance and the railroad tracks behind the hotel, while Jake worked on getting the other package out of locker number nine. Putting his fingers on the pressure release valve, he discovered it was stuck and wouldn't move, so the thing would never go off, unless it was given a stiff jolt. Relieved, he closed the locker and ran out to help Jesse, who was almost to the tracks. He yelled out, "The other bundle in eleven is harmless for now. Put that one between the tracks and head for cover."

Bernice was walking the halls when it hit her. *Why the hell didn't we think of this before? When Najib said it was easy to figure the room number, it was so simple we overlooked it. Shit!*

She got on the cell to Quint, who was walking the halls on another floor.

"Quint here."

"Quint, it's so simple we should have figured it out immediately." Bernice paused to get her breath back.

"Okay, I'll bite. What is so simple? We don't have time for riddles. Get on with it."

"When I was down the hall, the easy solution he was talking about came to me. After your conversation with Yancy, I remembered he said the locker at the bus depot was number nine and there was another locker involved. The lightbulb lit up. I'll bet the store that his room is on the ninth floor in room 911 or a room with the numbers 9 or 11. It will be easy enough to check out."

"Damn! You may have just grabbed the brass ring, Bernice. Let's take a quick recon of the ninth floor. I'll meet you there on the double."

"Okay, I'm on my way."

Bernice made it up to the ninth floor before Quint, and walked quietly down the hall checking room numbers. *BINGO! Damn, why didn't we figure this out before? Room 9011. All the numbers are there.*

She walked back down to the elevator just as Quint stepped off. "We have the right numbers, now we need to check who is registered in 9011."

Quint replied, "The house phone won't do us any good. The operators won't give out that information. I'll run back down to the front desk and drop a C-note on the shift manager. Be back in no time. Stand by until I return. We don't have much time, it's twenty to twelve."

While Quint was down checking with the front desk, Bernice walked back down the hall to the room and put her ear up to the door. All she could hear was the TV, with a news channel on. The sound was turned up enough for her to hear the newscaster reporting that there had been a huge explosion near the Plaza Hotel downtown. Her heart dropped, thinking of Jesse and Jake in the bus depot trying to defuse the bombs.

The reporter didn't know if or how many casualties there might be.

Bernice's blood started to boil, with thoughts of her partners spread all over the area of the blast. It was all she could do to keep from entering the room and shooting everybody inside.

She eased away from the door and returned to the elevator, praying they had the right room.

The elevator dinged as she was checking her weapon, hoping to empty it into the body of Mahathir.

"We have the right room," said Quint. "The clerk's description of Mahathir was right on."

"Did you feel an explosion a few minutes ago?"

"You know, I did get that pressure thing in my ears for a moment but didn't think much of it."

Bernice explained what she heard on the TV.

"Shit! I hope they had a controlled event. We can't worry about that right now. We've got our own problems on the front burner here. I'll call Sue, Keno, and Jett to get up here pronto. They are just a couple of floors down. Soon as they get here we'll decide on a plan of attack. Time is running out fast."

When Jake got out to the tracks Jesse was setting the bomb between the rails. "Jesse, we don't have much time. Drop the damn thing, and let's get as far away as we can. Come on!"

"Where's the other package?" asked Jessie.

"It's still in the locker. The valve is stuck; it won't go off without some help."

"Do you think when this goes off, it will trigger the other one?"

"It could, I guess. We don't have much to say about it right now."

As they were running towards the hotel, they saw two low-flying helicopters hit the twin towers of the Lady Luck Hotel and Casino.

Jake swore. "They must not have stopped all the choppers. Looks like we haven't done too well."

They ran into the parking garage's entrance. That would be the most stable place in an explosion.

After waiting for five minutes past the time the thing was supposed to go off, Jesse said, "Well, I wonder what the fuck's wrong now. Shit! I don't want to go back out there and check for a malfunction. I was in such a hurry, I didn't take a good look at it."

"I don't see a choice here. We have to go check it out," replied Jake.

"Okay, let's go."

When they got to the tracks, Jake said, "You remember when you were a kid on the Fourth of July, your fireworks didn't go off and you ran to check them, only to have them explode when you picked them up?"

"Yeah."

"Well, if that happens this time it won't just burn your fingers."

Jake carefully picked up the bomb, and Jesse shined his small pocket light on the device. They began to see what an amateur job had been done on its construction.

"No problem, Jesse. I see why the thing didn't go off."

246

"Okay, clue me in so my hands will stop shaking and my heart can get back to something near normal. I'm not into this bomb disposal stuff," replied Jesse.

"You don't get used to it, Jesse, you get tuned into it. Your focus is on the present, not what might happen, you leave that up to the Almighty."

"So, what's the fucking problem?"

"The timer is set for p.m. not a.m. It won't go off, if at all, until sometime after twelve noon."

"That's nice to hear. One problem out of the way. What about the one in the locker?"

"As far as I could tell, it won't go off without some assistance, which we have time to give it now. We'll take this back to the car and retrieve the other one. It's still a little tricky for us: we don't want to jar either of them."

"Okay, let's do it. I don't know how long my system can take this *MAYBE* shit. I like it a lot better taking chances with my own skills and not being on the ordnance disposal team."

After putting the bomb from locker eleven in the trunk, they returned to the bus depot. As they were walking from the garage to the depot, fire engines, cop cars of all sorts, ambulances, and every other type of emergency vehicle known to man were heading for or already at the Lady Luck, which was on fire and burning out of control.

"It looks like the helicopters had full tanks of fuel. This is one big-ass fire. Of all the fertile targets downtown, why did the dumbasses pick an empty hotel?" asked Jesse.

"Think about it a minute. What do the Lady Luck and the 9/11 attack have in common?" responded Jake.

Jessie pondered the question as they approached locker number nine. "I think I can answer that question without hesitation. The Lady Luck has twin towers. It's all symbolism."

"Right on. Now turn the key and open the locker. I'll try to lift the bomb out very carefully. Good thing about the helicopters: everyone is out in the street watching, and we can get this done without an audience."

The bomb came out easily, and they carried it gingerly back to the car, hoping the valve would not set itself free.

Jesse said, "You know these things could go off any time. Let's take them down to Bonneville Avenue. There's an underpass there. We can park the car, and if it goes off the explosion will go out either end of the underpass and up. It may not do nearly as much damage. There's a government building to the west, along with a shopping center that will be closed, and out the other side are some small businesses. The only one open is an adult book store. So we minimize the damage as best we can. We'll call Nellis Air Force Base, leave an anonymous tip about bombs in the underpass, and let the combat veterans defuse them."

"Sounds good to me. Let's go."

They drove the car south down to Bonneville and put the car sideways in the underpass, putting out flares to keep other cars away. With all the confusion downtown, it wouldn't seem out of place to see red highway flares directing traffic around an accident. The flares would last long enough for the Air Force to arrive.

Jake called the Nellis emergency number on his cell and told the operator about the car in the underpass laden with two bombs. They were already on high alert with news of the helicopters crashing into the Lady Luck.

Jesse said, "Well, we've done all we can here. Shall we hail a cab or steal a car and get back to the New York-New York?"

"Stealing a car might be quicker with all the confusion going on. I would prefer a Cadillac—you know, something made in America."

"Okay, a Cadillac it is."

With not so much as a how-do-you-do, Jesse had them riding towards the Strip in an Escalade in under ten minutes.

Chapter Twenty-one

Yancy

That fucking little voice won't leave me alone. Damn, I thought I was past that tear-jerking shit! I have to call Quint and silence that nagging intrusion in my life. Why can't I just be the person I am without all the drama? I may be evil in some eyes and not in others. Who's to say? I just want to go about life as I choose and let everyone else do the same. It's not any of my business what the rest of the world does. If they want to go on killing each other over some cockamamie idea about the afterlife, so be it. Is one man's God better than another's? If I don't believe in one or the other, do I go to paradise or hell, or is there only darkness? Only those who have made the trip know.

Yancy made the call.

"Quint here."

"Quint, I didn't share with you the whole story from Najib."

"You didn't tell me everything before, asshole. What the fuck did you leave out this time?"

"Some good news and some not so good."

"Get on with it, Yancy, we don't have time for your theatrics."

"Okay, you don't have to get so huffy. The plan for the New York-New York is only a diversion for something more sinister. The room is full of explosives, and they are on a clock set for 8:46, so you have time to take care of that. The other part is not so easy."

"Yancy, you are a lowlife son of a bitch."

"I know you don't like my way of thinking about life, but at this point that is not on the table. The fact that Hoover Dam is the main target should get your attention."

"You are a cockroach, Yancy. Slither in the dark, you fuck, after you spit out the details."

"No need to call me names, Quint, just because we see the world in a different light."

"If you were here right now, I would kill you. What made you come to Jesus all the sudden?"

"Jesus has nothing to do with my actions, which are none of your business. When you take your last breath, there will be only darkness. So, save your afterlife shit for someone else.

"Mahathir is not in the room. Just the explosives and the clock. He is out at Lake Mead getting his pontoon boat rigged for its journey to the dam. Actually there are two of them, one for each end of the dam. They think the ends are the weakest points, I don't know one way or the other, and I don't think they do either. It will be one hell of an explosion either way. The boats are at the Lake Mead Marina. Najib told me there is a lot of nitroglycerin on board, along with

C-4. The boats will breach the barrier strung across the expanse in the canyon just above the dam. Mahathir and the hapless fixed-wing pilot will sacrifice for the glory of Allah when they hit the concrete, unless of course you can send them on their way to the virgins before then."

"I don't suppose you have a bow number or slip space number?"

"Damn, Quint. I can't do everything for you. No, I didn't get those numbers. I was lucky to get what I got, with Najib thinking he was going to kill me the whole time he was spilling his guts. He was bragging big time about his goals for other people to do all the dying, while he was on his way to parts south with all the money he could ever want or need. All this happened just before I killed him. Which, I might add, did you a huge favor. You won't hear from me again."

Quint gathered the team at the end of the hallway by the elevator and brought them up to date, explaining Yancy's call.

"Okay, here's how it will go. Jake, Jett, Sue, Keno, and I will head out to the lake. We have some time before daylight to find the two pontoons. Bernice, you and Jesse get into Mahathir's room and see what you can do. Whether you can disarm the device or not, make an anonymous call to the Nellis emergency number, and then hightail it out to the lake."

After Quint and the others had boarded the elevator, Bernice said, "Okay, let's get into the room and see if we can defuse whatever is there and save the hotel."

Jesse said, "We can bribe the night housekeeper with a nice, crispy hundred dollar bill for a passkey. There also might be a problem with the door being booby-trapped, and I would hate to find out the hard way."

Bernice responded, "Let's go check things out before we decide to call for help."

"We could call Nellis first, and let them handle it."

"It's our job to take care of this, so let's quit pussy-footing around and get on with the program. We don't want to let anyone know what's up just yet. Let's take a look before we push the panic button."

Standing in front of the door to room 9011, Jesse observed, "The Do Not Disturb lock is on. You can only put that DND on from the inside. Yancy must have gotten some of his information confused, and there is someone in the room."

Bernice looked perplexed. "Yancy has been right about everything so far, even though he is a lowlife snake in the grass. There must be another way into the room."

Jesse exclaimed, "Hell, I know what's up! Damn, I should have hit on this right away. I bet this room is part of a suite, with connecting rooms. They put the lock on the door and then came out the connecting room. Let's get a passkey from the night maid."

The maid was in the supply room waiting for a call to touch up a room change or perform whatever task the front desk directed. With the encouragement of a hundred dollar bill, she loaned Jesse her passkey, but only if she came along.

When they opened the door, the connecting door to room 9011 was open.

Jesse gave the passkey back to the maid and told her to lose her memory of them and take a hike for her own safety. Pocketing her second hundred, she smiled and disappeared.

Bernice let out a low sigh as she observed the contents of room 9011. "Holy shit! There's enough C-4 in here to bring down most of this building, or at least destroy this side of the hotel. Look, the door is booby-trapped from top to bottom. If we had opened that door, it would have been our last curtain call. Damn!

"I think we'd better leave sleeping dogs lie and make another anonymous call to Nellis. I hope their guys know what the hell they're doing. This is some serious shit here."

"Bernice, Mahathir is not an explosives expert. I think Nellis would more likely blow themselves up trying to dismantle an amateur's mess than one made up by a pro."

Jesse got on the cell and called the emergency number for Nellis. When the operator answered, he said, "Room 9011 at the New York-New York is loaded with C-4 and who knows what else, all set to go off at 8:46 a.m. this very day. I suggest you get a team over here on the double. The room's door is booby-trapped; you'll have to go to the connecting room, number 9012."

Jesse heard a gasp as he ended the call. "I bet they are fit to be tied. I wonder how many teams they have to attack such emergencies?"

"Sir, we have another anonymous call about explosives," reported the operator. "The caller said a room in the New York-New York is laden with C-4 and other dangerous explosives. This is the third call. Sir, I believe we are under an attack similar to 9/11."

The officer of the day said, "Keep your thoughts to yourself. We don't know for sure what is happening."

The OD's cell barked. "Are you the OD?"

"Yes sir."

"I just returned home. What the hell is going on?"

"We are receiving anonymous calls. Two calls we received earlier turned out to be on target. We have engineers working on those.

"We just received another call about a problem at the New York-New York. I've dispatched our remaining engineers to that location. The Lady Luck was hit by two helicopters and is on fire. Fortunately the hotel is closed and there were no casualties. I believe it was a symbolic gesture similar to 9/11."

The commanding officer closed his cell and put in a secure call to the Joint Chiefs at the Pentagon.

Chapter Twenty-two

Hoover Dam

Bernice punched in Quint's cell.

"Yeah, Bernice, what's up?"

"We called Nellis to take care of the rooms at the hotel. It was a mess."

"Okay, come out to the Lake Mead Marina coffee shop."

"Ten-four, see you there."

"Jesse, we'll meet the team at the lake."

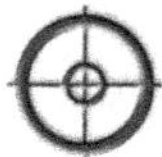

When they were all present in the coffee shop, Quint said, "We have to cover the whole marina and quickly. Hang out by the slip gate, I'll get a key."

Quint checked with the marina supervisor, showing him credentials of a border patrol agent, telling him they were looking for a couple of drug smugglers.

When the supervisor opened the gate, the team paired up and took loading carts through the gate, to make it appear they were resupplying their boats.

Sue and Bernice were almost to the end of the slips when Sue nearly walked into Mahathir and the fixed-wing guy, who were casting off their lines, preparing to push off. She waved at them and walked on past. Bernice was pulling the cart and turned around. She called Quint's cell and waved at Jake and Jett, who were on the other side of the slip, to come to her.

"Quint, we have found the boats. Sue walked past them as they were preparing to cast off. I have Jake and Jett's attention. We're at the last row of slips on the east side."

"Hold fast there, I'll get Keno and be right there."

Sue turned at the end of the dock and walked back towards Bernice. As she passed Mahathir, who was casting the stern line aboard his boat, she didn't notice the pilot come up behind her. He threw a gunny sack over her head and shoulders, pushing her onto Mahathir's boat. Mahathir jumped aboard and quickly bound a line around the gunny sack, securing it around Sue's legs, while the pilot released his own line and jumped onto his boat. With the lines off, the pilot guided his boat out of the slip towards the breakwater and the dam. Mahathir was not far behind.

Bernice was watching, but helpless to take any action, fearing they would pull the trigger on the boats and blow the whole marina up in smoke.

Bernice called Quint. "They've taken Sue!"

"Damn! How the hell did that happen? Shit!"

As they gathered near the end of the slip, the two pontoon boats were nearly out of the harbor's no-wake zone.

Quint gave rapid orders. "Jett, Jake, you guys go back to the van and drive up to the observation point near the dam checkpoint. When I send up a flare you pepper the boats with rifle fire until they blow up. Jesse, you and Keno find us a fast boat, so we can chase down the pontoons. Bernice, go back to the marina's maintenance building and get some flares."

Jesse and Keno brought the fast boat up to the slip, stopping long enough for Quint and Bernice to jump aboard.

"Okay, let's go fetch Sue and sink the pontoons."

Not paying any attention to the no-wake zone, Jesse took the boat out of the harbor at full throttle.

Quint typed in Jake's number. "Listen, when you get a chance, take out the pilot driving the lead pontoon boat. Hopefully, when he's down, the boat will come to a stop. We'll take on Mahathir from our end."

"Ten-four," answered Jake.

When they caught up to the two pontoons, they were nearly to the cliffs. Jesse steered the fast boat in between them, cutting off Mahathir from the pilot. Mahathir tried to flank the fast boat, but failed, ramming into them near the stern. The ramming turned both boats in opposite directions, giving Quint an opportunity to jump on board the pontoon.

Falling down as he landed, he did a somersault, coming up on his feet facing the wheelhouse, where Mahathir was shooting at him. The boat was still unsteady and his rounds went astray, not hitting anything.

Charging forward, Quint plowed headfirst through the plexiglas surrounding the wheelhouse, knocking Mahathir backwards over the captain's chair.

When they hit the deck, Mahathir's pistol went off. The bullet tore through his own head, killing him instantly. Quint rolled off his lifeless body. He looked frantically around for Sue, hoping she was not harmed.

He found her lying on the deck near the outdrive engine compartment.

"Sue, can you hear me?"

The gunnysack started flopping around as Sue tried to gain her freedom.

Quint told her, "Stop stirring around so I can release you. I don't want to cut your throat by mistake."

The sack became still and silent only long enough for Quint to cut her loose, and then the yelling began in earnest. "How did that son of a bitch know who I was? What the hell took you so long?"

Quint said, "Have you looked around? There are enough explosives on this boat to take out the whole fucking lake area."

"No, I haven't looked around. I've been in that sack since the docks. Jesus, we are sitting on something akin to nuclear!"

"You know, Sue, this is getting to be a habit I'm not enjoying. You put my life in danger every time we meet. Think we can find another way for us to find time together?"

"Cut the crap, Quint. What the hell are we going to do with this floating time bomb?'

"We are going to get on Jesse's fast boat and get as far away as we can. I'll signal Jake and Jett, who are up on the cliff there, to start peppering the boat until it blows up."

Jesse came alongside the pontoon boat, giving Keno a chance to help Sue and Quint aboard. They pulled away, heading in the opposite direction at full throttle. When they were a half mile away, Quint yelled for Bernice to shoot two flares.

Quint's cell barked as the flares went up. Jake's voice verged on frantic. "Quint, we took out the pilot, but he must have slumped over the throttle. The boat is heading for the dam wide open. He managed to make it around the end of the cliffs. The dam is a straight shot from there."

"Damn! Okay, we'll run him down. Disregard the flares. Hold your fire until we get around the end of the cliffs, then take out Mahathir's boat."

Quint yelled up to Jesse, "Come about, the lead boat is a runaway. We have to come alongside and board her."

Jesse brought the fast boat about, and at flank speed began the pursuit of the slow but steadily moving pontoon.

They closed with the pontoon quickly, then slowed to match her speed. The pilot was slumped over the controls, keeping the boat at full ahead. He was on his way to see the virgins without any of the fanfare he, Najib, and Mahathir thought they would receive for their sacrifice. No poems would be repeated over the years, for no one but the team would know who they were or how they died.

Jesse held the fast boat even with the pontoon, giving Quint and Keno an opportunity to jump aboard.

They were about to make their jump, when both boats began to rock and roll from the waves created as Jake and Jett's gunfire from the cliffs finally hit paydirt. The sound of the other pontoon boat exploding echoed off the walls of the narrow gorge leading to the dam.

Quint fell into the water as Keno hit the deck of the pontoon close to the wheelhouse. He rolled a couple of times and came up on his feet, only to hit the moving deck again.

The fast boat nearly capsized in the turbulent water, throwing everyone aboard to their knees, but Jesse was able to cut the engine to keep the props from finding Quint, who came up spitting water. He was able to grasp the cavitation plate to keep from getting crushed under the boat.

The boat continued its journey towards the dam as Keno got to his feet and managed to enter the wheelhouse and wrench the pilot from the controls. He pulled back on the throttle, only to find it was stuck on full ahead. Rushing back to the stern, he removed the cover hiding the boat's engine. With the boat still rocking, he pulled the fuel line from the carburetor, starving the engine into silence.

Returning to the wheelhouse, he stepped over stacks of C-4 and other explosives he wasn't sure about. With the engine noise gone, he could hear the ticking of a clock. Looking around he found the source of the ticking near the boat's head. The alarm was set for eight-twenty-four.

He had fifteen minutes to get off the boat and be as far away as possible.

The lake had settled down enough to fish Quint out of the water and make another try at disabling the pontoon. Jesse fired up the engine and steered toward the explosive-laden craft.

Bernice's cell buzzed for attention. "Bernice, you guys have fifteen minutes to pick me up and get us the hell out of Dodge. I don't have a clue how to disarm the array of explosives I'm sitting on, and the clock is set," exclaimed Keno. He sounded frantic.

"Quint, Keno is in big trouble." Bernce explained the situation word for word.

"Okay! Jessie, all ahead full, we have to pick Keno up ASAP and then get the hell out of the area. Bernice, call Jake and tell them to get back to the van and drive over to Temple Bar Marina. We'll meet them there. We need to disappear from here."

"Sir, another report just came in about a second explosion near the dam."

The officer of the day answered his cell after acknowledging the latest report. He heard the gruff voice of the commanding officer. "Did you get another report from the lake?"

"Yes sir."

"Do you have any more to share with me?"

"No sir. You know as much as I do, sir. We don't have a clue who is phoning in these reports or what exploded at the lake. The two explosions were minutes apart, with one fairly close to the dam, and the other not far behind. The park rangers didn't see anything unusual, but got a report of a boat leaving the dock area at full throttle from Lake Mead Marina. No one saw where the speeding boat went after it left the area. It's a mystery, sir."

The CO was getting reports that the engineers in the field had successfully disarmed all the bombs that were called in. It was not coincidence that the two helicopters chose to hit the empty Lady Luck Hotel.

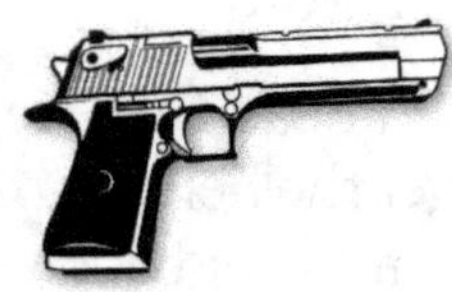

Chapter Twenty-three

Temple Bar

Jett drove the van to Temple Bar and the dock area, where Jesse had guided the fast boat into a slip.

The dock area was nearly a half mile from the marina's office, due to the lake dropping its water level over the past few years. Quint and the team were walking up to the restaurant when the van pulled up beside them. "Want a ride?" asked Jett.

"About time you got here. We've been waiting forever," replied Quint.

"Not true, Quint. We were parked up the hill waiting for you. Nice try."

The team, whole once more, gathered around the van shaking hands and congratulating each other on a job well done. Even though there had been some rough spots, the outcome was good.

Quint said, "We've saved a lot of lives over the past forty-eight hours, so we'll take our leave of this place and let the world try and figure out how the terrorist attacks were foiled. There will be no medals, Purple Hearts, or hearty handshakes from the saved. We know what happened, and that is all that matters. Keno, thanks for your help and if you don't mind, keep this adventure under your hat. You might think about filling a spot on our team."

"No thanks, guys. I've had my fill. Driving limos is just fine for me."

They piled into the van and headed back to the safe house to report the success of their mission to the Cabal and then disappear until there was another request for them to come to the aid of their country, a duty they would perform willingly as a team or individually, but on their terms, not on those of the bloated, politically correct, mindless masses in Washington, whose version of taking care of business involved the brain dead.

Quint asked Sue, "Do you have something in mind for this evening?"

"As soon as I heal up, I'll expect you to take me for cocktails, dinner, and dancing at our favorite place."

"Ten-four."

Chapter Twenty-four

The Pentagon

The Joint Chiefs were each handed a one-page letter.

FOR YOUR EYES ONLY

On 9/11, there were numerous planned attacks on the city of Las Vegas, Nevada and Hoover Dam. The attacks were thwarted with the help of God knows WHO. Those WHO gave us the location of planted explosives in three different hotels and those WHO also managed to stop an attack on the dam.

Engineers from Nellis AFB disarmed enough high explosives to take out the entire Las Vegas Strip. Two helicopters out of six survived an assault by the WHO, and managed to hit the Lady Luck Hotel, the only real damage done.

You are certainly aware of the above.

For now, I want to know who the WHO is that saved our asses. I want to know how they managed to have information we did not. We are supposed to have the largest and most efficient information-gathering system in the world.

I expect to have some answers, ASAP.

Secretary of Defense

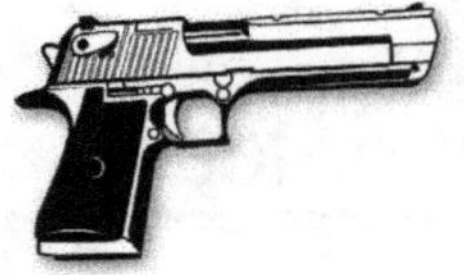

Chapter Twenty-five

Cabal Headquarters

Quint found himself sitting in the same chair that he'd sat in so many times before, but this time was different. There was only one person sitting opposite him. He handed Quint a one-page letter, then promptly rose and left the hall.

IT IS WITH GREAT PLEASURE THAT I CONGRATULATE YOU AND YOUR TEAM FOR AN OUTSTANDING PERFORMANCE IN LAS VEGAS.

THIS LETTER WILL DISINTERGRATE WITHIN FIVE MINUTES.

POTUS

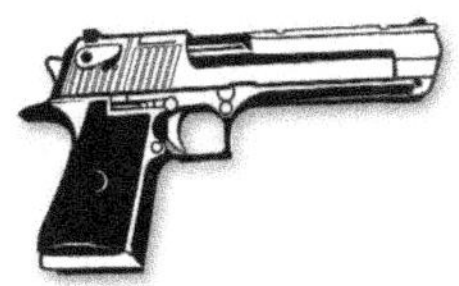

*"History does not entrust the care of freedom
to the weak or timid."*
Dwight D. Eisenhower

About the Author

    R. Michael Haigwood is a Marine Corps veteran,
life member of the Harley Owners Group (HOG),
and a lifelong resident of Nevada. He worked in the
Las Vegas gaming and hotel business for many years,
from the front of the hotel to the back end. He lives in
Henderson, Nevada with his partner, Jean.